LOVE

MARRIAGE

&

DIVORCE

NAVIGATING THE JOURNEY

UNRAVELING THE TRUTHS BEHIND

LOVE, COMMITMENT & SEPARATION

VICTOR IMHANS

"The greatest discovery of my generation is that a human being can alter his life by altering his attitudes of mind."

– Williams James

LOVE | MARRIAGE | DIVORCE

eBook ISBN: 979-8-9922777-0-8

ISBN: 979-8-9922777-1-5 (Paperback)

ISBN: 979-8-9922777-2-2 (Hardcover)

Printed in the United States of America.

CONTENTS

ACKNOWLEDGMENTS

Writing Love, Marriage, and Divorce: Navigating the Journey has been a happy experience, including love, education, and personal development. I am very happy for those who have supported me on this journey.

My family's support and encouragement have always been my backbone. To my beautiful children, thank you for your understanding, which has brought me happiness and inspired me.

To my friends and colleagues, I truly appreciate your support and positive perspective on this project.

I want to express my heartfelt appreciation to every couple who participated in this study and shared their stories with me. You have been sincere and open, and I am grateful to each one of you.

It would also be unfair not to acknowledge the researchers and experts who contributed their work and insights from relationship studies, psychology, and sociology to establish a strong foundation for this work on love, marriage, and divorce.

Finally, to all the readers out there, I would like to thank you for coming along with me on this journey. I hope this book will help as you go through your own journeys of love, marriage, and divorce.

With deepest gratitude,
Victor Imhans

FORWARD

L ove, marriage, and divorce are among relationships' most influential and life-changing events. Love, Marriage, and Divorce – Navigating the Journey is a touching account of these critical milestones in our lives, a guide to the phenomena they depict. Love is the primary feeling that makes our most fantastic dreams come true and adds joy and fire to our lives. This book is also a detailed account of the different aspects of love, from the first blush of enthusiasm to the more substantial and abiding affection that sees one through the various passes of one's living years. As one couple said, *"I never truly knew what love was before you came into my life."*

Marriage is a profound commitment that symbolizes a journey of shared growth, resilience, and deep emotional connection. It entails unique responsibilities that foster enduring bonds and mutual understanding. In 2022, approximately 2,065,905 marriages took place in the United States, resulting in a marriage rate of 6.2 per 1,000 people. This chapter on marriage offers valuable guidance for navigating challenges, enhancing communication, and embracing joyful moments. It highlights the importance of mutual respect, emotional intimacy, and shared experiences as the pillars of a successful partnership. A touching quote beautifully encapsulates this sentiment: *"Every day I tell you I love you, and it's true, today more so than yesterday and less so than tomorrow."*

Divorce is not an end but a new beginning—a chapter of healing, self-reflection, and growth. In 2022, there were approximately 673,989 divorces and annulments in the United States, yielding a national divorce rate of 2.4 per 1,000 people. Interestingly, about 43% of first marriages end in divorce, while the rates increase for subsequent marriages—60% for second marriages and 73% for third marriages. This book offers valuable guidance on navigating the emotional and practical challenges of divorce, empowering readers to embrace a renewed sense of freedom and purpose.

To make my point about the power of love, let me share a story I experienced. The first time I met a couple was when I learned they had been happily married for more than five decades now! Their love story began back in college with an act of kindness. On a day when the young man sitting next to her on the bus lent her his forgotten umbrella from home. Their initial interaction led to a conversation that eventually blossomed into a lifelong bond.

They went through so many changes in their lives, employment, and childbearing, but they never wavered in their love and commitment. *"We grew together, learned from each other, and never forgot how to laugh,"* they told me, and this, I believe, is an accurate depiction of love worth nurturing at any age.

Love, Marriage, and Divorce: Navigating the Journey is not just a fascinating book to read; it serves more as a vade mecum for anyone facing these significant milestones in their life. Divided into three central themes, this book provides the insight and encouragement that everyone needs as they pursue their own definitions of love, marriage, and divorce.

INTRODUCTION

When it comes to the diverse forms of human relationships, there is none as fulfilling as the phases of love, marriage, and divorce. Love, Marriage, and Divorce: Navigating the Journey is a heartfelt exploration of these pivotal stages in our lives, offering readers a roadmap to understanding and navigating their complexities. Love is the most basic emotional feeling that makes our greatest fantasies come true and adds happiness and passion to our lives. This book goes into the different aspects of love, from the worshipping stage to the companionship stage and all the stages in between. As one couple beautifully put it, *"Before you came into my life, I never felt love like this."*

Marriage, considered the most potent form of love, is a process of building a stronger relationship. It involves working to create a better and stronger home. Certain things are crucial for any marriage, including communication, conflict resolution, and intimacy. If necessary, addressing problems at the initial stage and seeking help from a professional is essential.

While divorce unravels a relationship, it is also a fresh start. Divorce involves personal healing, evaluation, and avoiding the same mistakes. Allowing oneself to mourn, grow, and enter into new relationships with healthier perspectives is important.

Thus, this journey reveals practical lessons on self-actualization, tenacity, and the wisdom of selecting the right life partner. It also sends out a message that divorce is not a stain but rather a chance for a fresh start and true happiness.

Understanding Love

To this end, love is discussed in various perspectives and their significant role in our daily lives. Love is an emotion of affection, intimacy, and passion, but it also has the components of caring, closeness, and commitment. It encompasses care, closeness, protectiveness, attraction, affection, and trust.

Love is one of the basic feelings omnipresent in culture and throughout humanity's existence on earth. It is the basis of our happiest and most fulfilling relationships and the reason for our happiest and saddest moments. Understanding the various types of love—romantic love, friendly love, family love, and others—helps one appreciate the variety of relations one has with other people.

This book will also explore the nature of love, romanticization, and the stages of couple relationships. It will address the essential factors for maintaining love, specifically communication and emotional intelligence.

The Realities of Marriage

The Realities of Marriage: Marriage is a continuous, dynamic journey that evolves through various stages, each presenting its own challenges and opportunities for growth. The initial phase is often marked by intense love and optimism. During this time, couples typically view their relationship through a romantic lens, experiencing heightened levels of intimacy, passion, and hope for the future.

Interference from families and friends: As the couple realizes they are no longer in the honeymoon phase, they begin to confront the challenges of sharing a home. This stage includes work-related adjustments, conflict resolution, and various other issues that are likely to arise when two people cohabitate. Couples create a schedule and, most importantly, develop a deeper understanding of each other. This phase is connected to establishing a strong and well-defined foundation for the relationship, which provides a sense of security.

If couples want to have children, this stage brings several new roles and responsibilities into the relationship. It can be hard to look after children, still have time for each other, and be a couple. When children grow up and leave home, the couples' relationships change somewhat. This stage is usually characterized by the rediscovery of each other and new hobbies that the couple has taken an interest in. With retirement, couples spend more time with each other, which is a blessing and a burden. This stage calls for changes in the schedule and changes in how people can have a good time during this part of life.

As people age, some of the things they have gone through in their marriage get to reflect on their journey and are ready to face other life changes, such as health issues. Rededicating the couple in marriage can be very fulfilling, particularly after many years. Rededication is about purposefully working to reconnect and enhance the relationship one has with one's significant other. It is a process accompanied by many challenges, such as the need to be patient, understanding, and growing together.

Knowing these stages will assist couples in managing their marriage more efficiently, anticipating problems, and enjoying happy moments. Each stage holds the potential to develop, grow closer, and be there for another person.

Marriage has long been one of the most meaningful connections between people, symbolizing love, commitment, and shared growth. However, sustaining a strong marriage requires effort, mutual respect, and dedication from both partners. This book explores the history and cultural significance of marriage, aiming to provide readers with a deeper understanding of its roots. It also examines essential components of a healthy relationship, such as open communication, conflict resolution, and practical problem-solving. Additionally, it addresses real-life challenges like financial difficulties and infidelity, offering thoughtful advice on recognizing and preventing these issues. Whether you're looking to strengthen your bond or simply gain a better understanding of marriage, this book is designed to guide you.

Divorce: A Survival Guide

Divorce can be quite a stressful and frustrating experience in anyone's life. Divorce is usually seen as a loss but also the beginning of a new life. Divorce is not only a legal process but also an emotional one, and it is essential to know the basics of the whole process. This book will help the reader deal with the emotional aspects of divorce, where to turn for support, and how to move on with one's life after a divorce. We shall also discuss how best to co-parent for the benefit of your children, as well as how to maintain healthy relationships with your ex-spouse.

Always remember that reaching out is important and taking it one day at a time is key. Each step toward the healing process is a step toward a better future.

A Self-Help Approach

This book is a theoretical analysis of love, marriage, and divorce and a practical self-help guide to help readers deal with these phenomena in their lives. Every chapter contains practical suggestions, cases, and exercises that can help readers assimilate the concepts of marriage described. Whether you want to understand love better after a divorce, this book is a practical guide that can help.

Embracing the Journey

Embracing the Journey of Love, Marriage, and Divorce means acknowledging the various stages of a relationship and the changes that occur. Throughout our lives, we experience various phases, sometimes marked by joy and other times by sadness. By exploring love, marriage, and divorce, we can gain a deeper understanding of the dynamics involved, thus equipping us to handle these situations more effectively. This book is a personal invitation to embrace the journey, cherish every experience that comes our way, and grow as individuals.

Therefore, it is crucial to engage in self-care, seek help when needed, and remain positive throughout this journey. All the phases bring lessons and possibilities for self-development, understanding oneself, and interactions with others. Welcome to Love, Marriage, and Divorce: Navigating the Journey. Now, let's embark on this journey with an open mind and heart, striving to better ourselves.

PART ONE

LOVE

Chapter 1

Love

Theories of love involve understanding how love develops, evolves, changes, and functions within relationships. Understanding these various theories provides valuable insights into relationship dynamics. Examining these theories can help us identify the key elements that contribute to a meaningful, balanced, and enduring bond. Psychologists and researchers present prominent perspectives to deepen our awareness of how love operates and thrives. Love is a complex emotion that deserves thorough understanding. Robert Sternberg's triangular theory of love categorizes love into three types that shape our relationships. This model can help us assess the health of our own relationships and pinpoint areas that may need attention or nurturing.

Intimacy: A sense of emotional closeness and deep connection.

Passion: The feeling of physical attraction and sexual desire.

Commitment: A conscious decision to maintain and foster the relationship over time.

Sternberg categorized love into three core components: intimacy, passion, and commitment. Various combinations of these components give rise to different types of love, including romantic love (a blend of intimacy and passion), companionate love (a mix of intimacy and commitment), and consummate love (which balances intimacy, passion, and commitment).

The Attachment Theory, first proposed by John Bowlby and later expanded by Mary Ainsworth, explores relationships among individuals, particularly the connections that develop in early childhood. The theory identifies several attachment styles: secure, anxious, and avoidant.

Secure Attachment: This attachment style is characterized by a profound sense of trust and safety in relationships, supporting the development of healthy and meaningful emotional connections.

Anxious Attachment: Characterized by feelings of uncertainty and anxiety, it often stems from unclear or inconsistent emotional bonds.

Avoidant Attachment: Characterized by a strong inclination to reduce emotional reliance on others, often resulting in discomfort with or avoidance of close emotional connections.

Attachment styles play a significant role in shaping adult relationships, particularly those focused on love and intimacy.

Psychologist John Lee developed the Color Wheel Theory of Love, linking various styles of love to specific colors on a wheel. He identified three primary love styles, which are as follows.

Eros: The romantic and passionate kind of love, focused on physical and emotional attraction.

Ludus: A playful and game-like type of love, often characterized by fun and casual relationships.

Storge: A love rooted in deep affection and friendship, more platonic than romantic in nature.

Lee described three secondary love styles that blend the primary ones. Pragma is a practical love focused on long-term compatibility. Mania is an intense, dramatic love with emotional ups and downs. Agape is a selfless, giving love centered on caring for others. These styles show how love can take on different forms in our relationships.

Compassionate vs. Passionate Love

Elaine Hatfield and her colleagues' classification of love into passionate and compassionate provides valuable insights into the nature of romantic relationships. Passionate love is defined by feelings of arousal, attraction, and a strong desire to be with the other person. It often involves idealizing the partner's qualities and experiencing a thrill in their presence. This type of love typically includes physical signs of arousal, such as an increased heart rate and 'butterflies in the stomach.' Although passionate love is intense, it is not permanent and can fluctuate unexpectedly.

Passionate love is characterized by intense emotions, physical attraction, and a yearning for closeness. It is often linked to physiological arousal, such as an increased heart rate and the familiar sensation of butterflies. While passionate love can be intense and appear enduring, it is also known for its tendency to fade. While it often dominates the early stages of a relationship, it is not unusual for it to diminish as the relationship evolves.

Compassionate Love

The type of love associated with compassionate love includes close emotional bonding, mutual respect, and a sense of closeness. It involves worrying about your partner's welfare and being there for them in times of need. This kind of love is built on trust, compassion, and a shared history of creating memories and attuning to each other's emotions and needs. It grows over the course of a relationship as the couple becomes more intimate. Regarding this, compassionate love tends to be more stable. It is often the primary feeling that couples have for each other after several years together, giving them the confidence that everything is well.

Compassionate love can help you cultivate a fulfilling and secure relationship. It prioritizes compassion, trust, and shared values to build a connection that grows over time, providing the comfort and unity to navigate life's challenges together. Making it a solid foundation that provides you with the strength to thrive, regardless of what comes your way.

Intensity vs. Stability

Passionate love is exhilarating and romantic, filled with intensity and excitement, but it can be unpredictable and may not always last. In contrast, compassionate love is steady, deep, and meaningful, forming the backbone of lasting and fulfilling relationships. Both play vital roles—passionate love ignites the initial spark and connection, while compassionate love nurtures and sustains the bond over time. By recognizing the balance and importance of these two types of love, we can better navigate our relationships and appreciate the value they bring at different stages.

Liking vs. Loving

Psychologist Zick Rubin observed that liking and loving are distinct emotional experiences. Liking is characterized by affection and admiration, while love delves deeper, involving emotions such as the longing to be close to the person you care for. According to Rubin's research identifies three key components through which love can be understood:

Attachment: The longing to be with another person.

Caring: It involves nurturing the other person's happiness and freedom.

Intimacy: Sharing personal feelings and thoughts.

These various theories of love provide different aspects of understanding love, showing that it is not a simple concept. Therefore, it is important to examine these theories to gain deeper insights into our various relationships and how we can improve them.

Loving Yourself

If you do not love yourself, how can you love others? Self-love is the understanding and appreciation of oneself in a manner that enhances one's well-being. It is an affection for oneself, which entails self-respect, self-esteem, and self-compassion. Self-love is the acceptance of oneself and the appreciation of oneself as one would appreciate a friend.

Self-love can be beneficial in the prevention of stress, anxiety, and depression. It fosters strength and optimism, as well as a good self-image. When one is loving, one is more likely to take proper care of one's body through proper diet, workout, and enough sleep. Self-love also enhances one's interpersonal relationships. When one is confident, one is able to draw healthy personal boundaries and have healthy interpersonal relationships. Learn to treat yourself with the same affection and compassion you would treat a friend. This implies being gentle to oneself in times of failure or hardship.

It involves engaging in activities that benefit the body, mind, and spirit. These could include interests, fitness routines, meditation, or leisure time. Negative thinking can be transformed into positive affirmations, and practicing gratitude for the good things in life can shift the focus from lacking what one desires to appreciating what one has. Self-love is a journey and an ongoing commitment in one's life, and it is not a static concept. It is a decision-making process that integrates attention to one's needs into everyday life.

Chapter 2

Biological and Psychological Aspects of Love

L ove is one of the most complex and rewarding feelings, and it is also influenced by psychological and biological factors. Love is not just a feeling that we experience in our minds. It is an actual physical experience that affects our body through hormones, neurotransmitters, and specific areas of the brain. Let's look at the following key players and their roles in the experience of love.

Integrating the concepts of love and psychological states, the idea of love as a psychological experience highlights a rewarding journey that fosters personal growth and the development of meaningful relationships. It promotes mutual fulfillment and intimacy. Love influences emotions, decision-making, and behavior within a relationship. Recognizing the connection between psychological and biological aspects enhances well-being. It illustrates how the highs and lows of love contribute to psychological insights alongside biological challenges, ultimately nurturing a genuine emotional experience as the brain interacts with various reinforcing biological emotions. This enriches our understanding of love's intricate mental, emotional, and physiological dimensions. Biological insights provide diverse perspectives, enabling us to cultivate deeper, more resilient relationships and grasp the fundamental biological foundations of chemistry.

Let's focus on the basics of love and relationships for now. We can explore more complex details about how the brain works and processes love later. Starting with the foundations will make everything easier to understand and put into practice. In understanding the emotional process, two fundamental needs stand out as vital for achieving biological and psychological fulfillment in life. Love, whether viewed as an emotional phenomenon through developmental processes or not, activates corresponding chemical reactions within us.

From this perspective, understanding how these thoughts cultivate a deep and lasting connection allows us to engage more fully. This essence provides an experience that relates not only to a specific place but also to an understanding that promotes self-disclosure, driven by a holistic view that creates meaningful insights into love and the self. In this intricate dynamic, psychological behaviors and strategies contribute to maintaining connections supported by neurotransmitters that nurture love within us. The pursuit of healthy relationships involves navigating the profound emotional experiences vital to romantic bonds, guiding us toward richer experiences.

Understanding how biology influences love and connection provides valuable insights into the natural processes that shape human relationships. We can better comprehend the emotions and behaviors that foster bonds by exploring the roles of hormones, neurotransmitters, and evolutionary mechanisms. This knowledge not only deepens our appreciation for love's complexity but also equips us with greater awareness to navigate and nurture meaningful relationships.

Oxytocin and Vasopressin

Oxytocin and vasopressin are chemicals often called the "love hormones" because they are involved in bonding and attachment. Oxytocin is released during affectionate activities like hugging, kissing, and sexual intercourse. This hormone is linked to feelings of affection, trust, and emotional connection, strengthening the bond between partners. Similarly, vasopressin is connected to behaviors that encourage the formation of long-term bonds.

Role: Oxytocin and vasopressin play crucial long-term roles in the development of relationships. Oxytocin is secreted during touch and intimacy and is associated with feelings of trust. Vasopressin is connected to behaviors that help maintain bonds, such as pair bonding and monogamy.

Impact: These hormones facilitate the transition from the tumultuous phase of infatuation to a stronger bond. They enhance emotional connection and feelings of security, which are essential for the sustainability of relationships.

Bonding and Attachment: Oxytocin, commonly known as the love hormone or cuddle hormone, is released during activities such as hugging, kissing, and sexual intercourse. It fosters feelings of intimacy, trust, and emotional connection between partners.

Maternal Behavior: Oxytocin plays a crucial role in mother-infant bonding. It is released in large quantities during labor and breastfeeding to facilitate bonding between the mother and the infant newborn.

Stress Reduction: Oxytocin and cortisol levels can help alleviate stress and anxiety by calming the body. This creates a relaxing effect and enhances feelings of comfort and security.

Monogamous Behavior: Vasopressin is linked to behaviors that encourage long-term fidelity between partners. It contributes to pair bonding, especially in males.

Protective Behavior: This hormone is linked to protective and possessive behaviors that can strengthen and solidify a relationship.

Dopamine

Dopamine functions as both a neurotransmitter and a hormone, playing a crucial role in various bodily functions. This neurochemical is closely linked to the experience of falling in love, influencing its levels across different stages of the relationship. By triggering feelings of happiness and excitement, dopamine enhances pleasure and enjoyment, creating an intense emotional response. This surge of positivity often drives individuals to seek out the experience repeatedly, reinforcing the connection.

Role in Pleasure and Reward

Role: At the beginning of the relationship, dopamine and norepinephrine levels rise, leading to feelings of happiness and pleasure. These neurotransmitters play a key role in the so-called 'honeymoon phase,' when everything about the partner appears terrific.

Euphoria and Excitement: Dopamine is a neurotransmitter that plays a crucial role in the brain's reward system. It is the chemical associated with feelings of happiness, excitement, and other positive emotions commonly experienced during the falling-in-love phase.

Motivation and Desire: Dopamine is the neurotransmitter that fuels interest, encouraging individuals to pursue rewarding experiences, such as spending time with a partner. It amplifies behaviors associated with pleasure and happiness.

Serotonin

Serotonin is another neurotransmitter that significantly influences romantic mood, love, and behavior in the early stages. Studies have indicated that lower serotonin levels may lead to obsessive thinking and an increased focus on one's partner. This phenomenon resembles obsessive-compulsive disorder, and one might argue that love is similar to it, with serotonin levels often feeling intense and sometimes overwhelming.

Role in Mood Regulation

Role: Research indicates that serotonin levels decrease during the obsessive early thinking phase and the intense focus on falling in love with a partner.

Impact: This decrease in serotonin heightens individuals' awareness of their partner, intensifying their passion for the new relationship.

Mood and Obsessive Thoughts: Serotonin is a neurotransmitter that regulates mood, appetite, and sleep. In the early stages of romantic love, serotonin levels may drop, potentially explaining the obsessive thoughts and intense focus on the partner.

Emotional Stability: Research indicates that normal serotonin levels correlate with healthy emotional functioning and overall well-being. While excess serotonin usually has little effect on the body, low serotonin levels can result in various mood disorders, including depression and anxiety.

Endorphins

Endorphins are Endorphins are natural chemicals produced by the brain and nervous system. They act as the body's built-in pain relievers and mood boosters. By blocking pain signals and creating feelings of happiness or well-being, endorphins help us feel better both physically and emotionally. The name *"endorphin"* comes from the term *"endogenous morphine,"* highlighting that they're made by the body and work similarly to morphine. These powerful hormones play an essential role in reducing pain and lifting our mood.

The Role of Endorphins in Physical and Mental Health

Endorphins play an important role in regulating pain and providing relief to the body. They are released in response to stimuli such as exercise, laughter, and sexual activity. Physical activity, especially high-intensity workouts, is known to trigger the release of endorphins, which can lead to a *"runner's high"* and reduce the perception of pain. Additionally, endorphins contribute to feelings of satisfaction and reward, reinforcing positive behaviors such as exercise and social interaction.

In addition to their pain-relieving properties, endorphins also affect mood and emotions. They are released during times of happiness and well-being, enhancing a sense of contentment and joy. This is why endorphins are often pursued through activities that foster happiness and well-being, such as spending time in nature, engaging in creative endeavors, or cultivating social relationships.

Research indicates that endorphins can boost cognitive function and enhance mental clarity. They play a critical role in processes such as decision-making, problem-solving, and memory formation, assisting individuals in navigating complex situations more easily. Additionally, endorphins can stimulate the brain's reward centers, fostering a sense of satisfaction while increasing motivation and focus.

Some studies suggest that endorphins might have anti-inflammatory properties and contribute to immune system function. While the mechanisms behind these effects are not entirely understood, endorphins could help promote overall health and resilience against illness.

Endorphins Benefits on Mood and Emotional Well-Being

Regular endorphin release can enhance mood and emotional well-being. When released, endorphins foster feelings of euphoria or relaxation. This is one reason why activities that promote happiness, such as laughing, socializing, or attending events, boost self-esteem and confidence. Endorphins are also released when individuals achieve personal goals and take pride in their accomplishments. Engaging in physical activities helps manage stress, leading to a sense of happiness and contentment in life.

How to Increase Endorphin Levels

Engaging in regular physical activity is one of the most effective ways to boost endorphin levels. Exercise, especially high-intensity workouts, and endurance training has been shown to trigger the release of endorphins, which can improve mood and reduce the perception of pain. Other forms of physical activity, such as yoga and Pilates, can also enhance endorphin levels, as they promote relaxation and reduce stress.

Meditation and other mindfulness practices stimulate the release of endorphins, which help reduce stress and enhance mental well-being. By focusing on breathing and being present, individuals can activate this endorphin response, fostering a sense of calm and tranquility. Likewise, laughter—whether it arises from humor, comedy, or social interactions—acts as a well-documented trigger for endorphin release, improving mood and emotional welfare.

A healthy diet can also influence endorphin levels, with foods high in tryptophan, an amino acid involved in producing endorphins, being particularly beneficial. Foods such as turkey, eggs, and legumes are rich in tryptophan and can help support endorphin production when included in a balanced diet. Additionally, omega-3 fatty acids found in foods like salmon, flaxseeds, and chia seeds have been shown to have a positive impact on mood and may indirectly influence endorphin levels.

Some supplements, such as omega-3 fatty acids and magnesium, may also help increase endorphin levels. However, it is important to consult with a healthcare professional before taking supplements, as different factors, such as dosage and individual health status, may affect their safety. A low level of endorphin effectiveness may pose potential risks, resulting in various adverse health effects.

Testosterone and Estrogen

Testosterone and estrogen are hormones that are essential for keeping our bodies healthy and functioning properly. Although they may be associated with different genders, they are important for everyone.

Testosterone is mainly produced in the testes for men and, in smaller amounts, in the ovaries for women. Both men and women also make small amounts of it in their adrenal glands. Often linked to male traits, like facial hair and muscle growth, testosterone is much more than that—it also helps with energy, mood, and even libido in both men and women.

Estrogen, meanwhile, is a group of hormones essential for women's health, particularly their reproductive system. The three main types—estrone (E1), estradiol (E2), and estriol (E3)—each have distinct roles. Most estrogen is produced by the ovaries, although smaller quantities are also synthesized in the adrenal glands and fat tissues. Estrogen is crucial for regulating the menstrual cycle and for maintaining strong bones, heart health, and physical characteristics such as breast development. While it's often referred to as a "female hormone," men also require small amounts of estrogen to support bone density and reproductive health.

Both hormones are essential for physical and emotional health, working in concert to maintain balance and promote thriving. When their levels align, they support everything from strength and vitality to reproduction and overall well-being. These small chemical messengers significantly influence our growth, feelings, and everyday lives.

Role in Sexual Attraction and Behavior

Sexual attraction significantly influences human behavior, interactions, relationships, and social dynamics. It often serves as a driving force behind emotional connections and decision-making in various contexts.

Role: Testosterone and estrogen are connected to libido and sexual desire.

Impact: Although testosterone and estrogen are important, they are linked to the relationship between these mood hormones and emotional well-being. Maintaining a healthy balance of these hormones is crucial for ensuring sexual intimacy and overall relationship satisfaction.

Sexual Desire: Libido and sexual attraction are influenced by testosterone, which occurs in both men and women, although men typically have it at higher levels.

Reproductive Health: On the other hand, estrogen is primarily produced in women and plays a crucial role in reproductive health and sexual function. It also affects mood and emotional well-being.

Cortisol

Cortisol is a hormone produced by the adrenal glands, which are located atop the kidneys. It plays a significant role in various bodily functions, primarily in the stress response. As an essential steroid hormone, cortisol helps manage stress. It is released in the presence of a stressor, triggering a series of events that allow you to cope with that stressor.

Some changes that occur include elevated blood sugar levels, increased mental efficiency, and the suppression of other systems, like the digestive and immune systems, allowing the body to confront the stressor. Additionally, cortisol not only helps manage stress but also regulates metabolism, reduces inflammation, and supports memory formation. It is essential for various bodily functions, particularly in the body's response to stress.

Cortisol is the most prevalent hormone released by the body. During conflict or in response to stress, cortisol levels may increase, causing tension and anxiety, which can lead to a heightened emotional response. Stress and cortisol are known to negatively affect relationships, while relaxation and bonding practices like touch and communication can help reduce cortisol levels and anxiety.

Psychological Impact

Love isn't simply about feelings—it profoundly influences our mental and physical health. Beyond biology, love can enhance our happiness, provide a sense of fulfillment, and offer essential emotional support. It also helps protect us from stress, providing comfort and stability during difficult times. Physically, the positive emotions associated with love can result in lower blood pressure, an improved immune system, and even a decreased risk of certain chronic illnesses. Love truly nurtures both the heart and mind.

The Role of Oxytocin in Bonding

Let's consider Anna and Rob, a couple who have been together for over twenty years. They occasionally express physical affection by holding hands, hugging, and cuddling. These intimate gestures release oxytocin in their bodies, which strengthens their emotional bond and provides a sense of security. This biological process enhances their psychological intimacy, making them feel closer and more at ease with each other.

Hormones play a significant role in shaping the dynamics of relationships at various stages of a person's life. From the initial thrill of infatuation to the enduring bonds of marriage, these biochemical agents influence our moods, behaviors, and interactions with our significant others. Therefore, it is crucial to understand that being aware of hormones can help us navigate the different phases of a relationship and strengthen our connections.

This process also helps us understand the biological aspects of love, allowing us to comprehend the phenomenon more thoroughly. Love is not merely a feeling; it is a complex network that influences our thinking and physical well-being, shaping our experiences and interactions. This understanding can help us nurture and maintain love, ultimately leading to better and stronger relationships.

Love is a powerful emotion that shapes how we feel, think, and act. It has the incredible ability to lift our spirits, boost our confidence, and help us better handle stress and illness. Love is not just something we feel—it's a state of being that impacts every part of our lives.

How Does Aging Affect Hormones in Relationships

Aging impacts hormones in various ways, which can influence relationships differently. As mentioned previously, hormone levels change over time, affecting both the emotional and physical dimensions of relationships. Here's a summary of how aging affects key hormones and their role in relationships.

Estrogen and testosterone are sex hormones that play crucial roles in physical and emotional well-being. They are vital for fertility, libido, mood, and overall health. A decline in estrogen and testosterone levels as people age can lead to changes in physical appearance and libido, potentially affecting the desire for intimacy. These hormonal changes can also impact the emotional connection among older adults.

Oxytocin is often called the *"cuddle hormone"* because it promotes bonding and attachment. It is released during physical contact, such as hugging or cuddling, and is crucial in developing emotional connections with partners. However, aging can affect the production of oxytocin, complicating the emotional aspects of relationships.

DHEA (dehydroepiandrosterone) is a hormone produced by the adrenal glands. Its levels generally decrease with age. DHEA is linked to energy, mood, and overall well-being. A reduction in DHEA can result in feelings of low energy and reduced vitality, which may impact relationship dynamics.

Thyroid hormones are crucial for metabolism and energy levels. Imbalances in the thyroid, which can affect sexual desire, significantly impact cellular repair and healing times, ultimately reducing energy levels and affecting the overall quality of relationships. Vasopressin is also linked to social behaviors. Changes in weight interaction can, in turn, influence tissue gain, leading to a decrease in dopamine and pleasure. A lower level of desire and overall enjoyment associated with the hypothalamus-pituitary-gonadal (HPG) axis involves vasopressin function, and individuals produce emotional neurotransmitters that regulate hormones. Disruptions in this axis can result in low dopamine levels during physical intimacy. This aspect of production can influence energy, and activity related to these changes plays a significant role.

The Hypothalamus Pituitary Adrenal (HPA) axis plays a crucial role in regulating stress response and cortisol levels. As people age, the body may become more sensitive to cortisol, resulting in heightened stress responses to minor stressors. Chronic stress can adversely affect both physical and emotional health, potentially impacting the quality of relationships.

Hormones such as insulin, leptin, and ghrelin also affect energy metabolism, appetite, and sensations of fullness. Imbalances in these hormones can result in weight gain and decreased energy levels, which may subsequently impact relationship dynamics.

Older adults must address hormonal imbalances through appropriate medical interventions to enhance their overall health and improve the quality of their relationships.

While hormonal changes are a natural part of aging, they do not have to indicate the end of intimacy or emotional connection. Many older adults continue to enjoy intimate relationships by adapting and discovering innovative ways to connect. For example, they can engage in non-sexual activities that promote emotional bonding, such as shared hobbies, discussing their day, or exploring new experiences together. These activities can strengthen the emotional foundation of the relationship.

Physical contact, like holding hands or offering gentle touches, can provide comfort and connection for older adults. These simple gestures promote a sense of calm and reassurance, strengthening the emotional bond between partners. When mobility becomes challenging, older adults can adjust their routines to include more rest periods or explore alternative forms of intimacy, such as cuddling or sharing their feelings. This helps maintain the emotional connection and ensures that both individuals feel comfortable.

Diet and exercise play vital roles in managing hormonal balance, particularly for older adults. Maintaining a healthy diet that includes fruits, vegetables, lean proteins, unprocessed foods, and whole grains supports hormone production and promotes overall well-being. Furthermore, regular physical activity helps regulate hormone levels, boosts mental health, and enhances quality of life.

Tackling these challenges will enhance your daily mood and establish a solid foundation for healthier, more meaningful relationships. Whether you're taking small, manageable steps like practicing mindfulness, cultivating self-compassion, or relying on trusted friends for support, every effort adds up. Over time, these positive changes foster a sense of balance and connection, enriching your personal growth and the relationships you cherish most.

As people age and experience changes that impact their connections and physical closeness, relationships can develop through understanding, openness, and professional support. Sustaining love and affection necessitates adaptability and continuous care to endure the challenges of time.

Love, throughout the years, is a personal and complex concept influenced by individual experiences as well as cultural and societal norms regarding beliefs about aging. As individuals progress through different phases of life, the dynamics of love and relationships may shift, presenting both challenges and opportunities for personal growth and deeper connections with others.

Love in later life can take many forms, including romantic relationships, marriages, enduring friendships, and supportive connections with family and community. Although aspects of romantic relationships in older adulthood have been examined, research on love in other types of relationships, such as friendships and non-romantic connections, remains limited. This underscores the need for a more nuanced understanding of how love manifests in later life and how these various forms contribute to overall well-being and quality of life.

Overall, the quote *"Love is ageless"* underscores the lasting power of love across generations. It emphasizes the significance of empathy, understanding, and support in cultivating meaningful relationships and fostering a more cohesive and caring society. By nurturing love and support over time, we can create a more interconnected, compassionate, and fulfilling experience for everyone involved. This offers valuable insights and inspiration for individuals, families, and communities to embrace the timeless beauty of love and connection.

Navigating Hormonal Changes in a Long-Term Relationship

Consider a couple, John and Mary, who have been married for twenty-five years. As they entered their 50s, both experienced changes in their physical and emotional well-being. John had low testosterone levels, which are linked to decreased energy and sexual drive. Menopause affected Mary, leading her to cope with hot flashes and mood swings. Consequently, Mary's hormonal imbalance significantly impacted her estrogen levels.

To cope with these changes, John and Mary focused on maintaining open communication and supporting one another. They sought medical advice to manage their symptoms and incorporated lifestyle changes such as regular exercise, a healthy diet, and stress-reducing activities like yoga and meditation. They also tried to maintain physical affection and spend quality time together, which helped sustain their emotional connection and intimacy.

Understanding these changes and their consequences enables individuals to navigate this stage of life with sensitivity and compassion. By practicing open communication, encouraging medical intervention when necessary, and nurturing emotional and physical connections, couples can strengthen and enrich their relationships as they age.

Lifestyle Changes to Help with Hormonal Balance

The body utilizes hormonal balance to regulate essential functions such as healthy growth, mood, individual metabolism, and reproductive processes. Disparities can result in various complications, including weight issues, fatigue, mood swings, and more severe conditions such as diabetes and thyroid disorders. For instance, menopause in women and low testosterone in men can impact libido and sexual function. Women might experience vaginal dryness or discomfort, while men may have difficulty maintaining an erection. These are typical concerns and addressing them with care and understanding can lead to meaningful improvements.

Certain chronic diseases affecting the joints, diabetes, and heart conditions can render sexual activity challenging or uncomfortable. Additionally, some medications prescribed for high blood pressure and mood disorders may have side effects that diminish sexual drive and performance.

Certain conditions can arise from aging, including low self-esteem and poor body image, which may lead individuals to feel unattractive and undesirable. Intimacy fosters a unique emotional bond between partners, which strengthens feelings of love, trust, and closeness. Studies also indicate that being in a relationship can positively impact one's health, including reducing stress, boosting the immune system, and enhancing overall well-being. Additionally, intimacy may support mental health by helping to combat feelings of loneliness and depression while couples experience increased happiness and satisfaction in their intimate lives. Research on relationships shows that higher-quality connections lead to greater satisfaction levels.

Here are some tips that can assist in changing lifestyle habits to enhance hormonal balance.

Getting Enough Sleep

Importance: Sleep is crucial for stabilizing hormone levels. Insufficient sleep can seriously affect hormone balance, including cortisol, insulin, and growth hormone.

Tips: Aim for 7-9 hours of quality sleep each night.

Establish a relaxing routine before bedtime, avoid screens before sleeping, and ensure your sleeping environment is calm and completely dark.

Managing Stress

Importance: Stress is a significant issue as it increases cortisol levels, which in turn affects our hormones.

Tips: Practical stress management methods include meditation, yoga, deep breathing, and spending time outdoors. Living an active lifestyle while making time for calming moments boosts energy, restores balance, and enhances overall well-being, paving the way to a healthier, more fulfilling life.

Regular Exercise

Importance: It also helps control hormones that regulate hunger, energy storage, and stress.

Tips: Engaging in aerobic exercises, strength training, and stretching is advisable. Surprisingly, even brief, regular workout sessions can be quite beneficial.

Healthy Diet

Importance: A balanced diet is essential for maintaining normal hormonal secretion.

Tips: Eat healthy foods, such as fruits, vegetables, proteins, and healthy fats. Limit your consumption of sugar and heavily processed foods. Omega-3 fatty acids, which are found in fish, flaxseeds, and walnuts, are known for their positive effects.

Improving Intimacy with Old Age

Yes, it is true that as couples age, keeping the spark alive can be challenging, or as people say, 'the marriage bed gets colder.' However, it's possible to rekindle that connection with some effort and understanding. Here are some strategies to help:

Open Communication

Importance: Couples need to express themselves and share their feelings, desires, or thoughts to strengthen their bond.

Tips: Communicating openly and listening to your partner without criticism. Approach discussions about any issues or changes in sexual interest with sensitivity.

Physical Affection

Importance: Showing affection includes loving acts such as hugging, kissing, and holding hands, which can elevate oxytocin levels in the body and strengthen the connection between individuals.

Tips: Simple, non-sexual touch can powerfully nurture intimacy and strengthen the connection between partners, especially as they navigate physical changes together. It's a small gesture with a significant impact.

Adapt to Physical Changes

Importance: Some changes that happen with aging include decreased libido, erectile dysfunction, and vaginal dryness, among others

Explore different ways to be intimate that are comfortable for both partners. For vaginal dryness, using lubricants can be beneficial, while other issues, such as erectile dysfunction, should be discussed with a doctor.

Prioritize Emotional Intimacy

Importance: Emotional intimacy is a profound sense of closeness and connection that transcends physical interactions. It is built on shared understanding, trust, and emotional vulnerability, forming a deep and meaningful bond.

Spending meaningful time together, engaging in shared interests, and providing emotional support are powerful ways to deepen the bond between partners. Building an emotional connection can also positively influence and enrich the physical relationship

Stay Healthy Together

Importance: Maintaining good physical health is vital for overall well-being and key to a satisfying sexual life. By prioritizing regular exercise, balanced nutrition, quality sleep, and stress management, partners can enhance their energy levels, mood, and confidence. A healthy lifestyle strengthens the body and deepens emotional and physical intimacy, enriching the relationship.

Tips: Regular health check-ups are recommended to identify and address any medical concerns that might impact intimacy. Engaging in exercise, following a balanced diet, and managing stress are also beneficial for maintaining a healthy and fulfilling relationship.

Maintaining Intimacy in Later Years

For instance, consider Linda and Robert, a couple married for thirty years. Now in their early sixties, they have noticed changes in their sex drive and physical strength. To maintain intimacy in their relationship, they prioritize communication and regularly discuss their needs and concerns. They also occasionally engage in physical affection, such as holding hands and cuddling. Moreover, they have adapted their physical intimacy, explored various forms of closeness, and sought medical assistance when necessary.

Therefore, Linda and Robert, who closely focused on the emotional aspects of their relationship and made a concerted effort to maintain their health, were able to keep the spark alive. Managing hormones and intimacy becomes increasingly important as one ages, and these factors contribute to that goal. With these adjustments, couples can improve their overall health and find themselves better positioned to nurture a fulfilling and intimate relationship.

Falling in Love

Romantic relationships naturally progress through different stages, evolving as couples experience various milestones. Falling in love is often viewed as a multi-stage process, with each stage presenting distinct characteristics. Understanding these stages, couples can more effectively navigate the challenges unique to each phase and cultivate a deeper connection and intimacy along the way.

While popular culture often romanticizes the experience of falling in love, the reality is much more complex. This journey unfolds through distinct stages: the initial spark of attraction, the excitement of new love, the commitment needed to maintain a relationship, and the growth that arises from shared experiences. Let's explore the recurring themes that shape and define the process of falling in love over time.

Chapter 3

Love At First Sight

Love at first sight describes an instantaneous feeling of affection that arises without a clear explanation. This concept suggests that love can develop quickly, often driven by impulse. This immediate and intense attraction to someone, typically lacking rational reasoning or understanding, can grow rapidly, fuelled by instinct and chemistry.

From initial meetings to falling in love, romantic relationships usually start with attraction and curiosity. They naturally progress from the thrill of early dates to the decision to commit. Friendships can certainly evolve into romantic relationships as long as there is mutual attraction and interest. Keeping spontaneity alive in relationships is possible through intentional efforts to ensure things remain exciting and fresh.

Effective trust and communication create essential emotional connections. This in turn, stresses the significance of transparency in creating closeness and dealing with conflicts. It is possible to state that long-distance relationships can be as strong and healthy as the relationships where the partners live nearby and can meet more often. It just requires some techniques, and both the parties involved must be willing to make it work. The challenges of maintaining connections across distances offer valuable insights into managing them effectively. Taking time to slow down in relationships can be advantageous, allowing individuals to develop intimacy and understanding at a natural pace.

Cultural and societal norms play a significant role in determining the expectations and actions that are considered normal in romantic relationships. It is important to recognize how various cultures define love, marriage, and commitment and how society's perspective on these aspects has changed. Trust is the building block of a healthy relationship, as it allows for dependence, openness, and emotional closeness. Every couple needs to communicate effectively for the two partners to feel listened to, trusted, and close.

Attraction

The first stage of emotional attraction occurs when you find someone appealing. During this initial phase, you may feel a buzz or butterflies in your stomach as you develop affection for that person. This stage is often triggered by physical appearance.

Factors such as a smile, eyes, or an overall attractive look can contribute to this feeling. Qualities that make a person more likable include kindness, confidence, humor, intelligence, and many other traits. Shared interests encompass common hobbies and passions that people may enjoy or believe in.

Infatuation

Infatuation is an intense emotional and passionate attraction toward someone, often occurring in the early stages of a connection. It is marked by a thrilling sense of euphoria, excitement, heightened desire to be close to the person, and feelings of lust, idealization, and obsessive thoughts. During this stage, the individual may appear flawless, as infatuation amplifies their positive traits while downplaying or ignoring imperfections. This often leads to persistent thoughts about them and a strong urge to be in their presence. While the experience can be exhilarating, it may also feel overwhelming or stressful due to the unpredictability and intensity of emotions involved. From an expert perspective, infatuation is a natural and often essential step in forming deeper relationships, creating the initial spark that can evolve into mature love through trust, understanding, and acceptance of imperfections. By moving beyond the idealized perception of another person and concentrating on emotional intimacy and shared values, individuals can turn infatuation into a meaningful and lasting bond that balances passion with authentic connection. This insight empowers us to take control of our emotions and relationships, leading to a more fulfilling and enduring experience bond.

Attachment

As the relationship evolves, partners cultivate their emotions and strengthen their trust. Attachment acts as the foundation of the relationship, providing the support necessary to navigate challenges and encourage ongoing growth.

This stage involves:

Emotional Connection: A deep affection and a strong sense of comfort define your bond with your partner.

Trust and Dependence: At this stage, both of you become more interdependent in terms of emotional intimacy and affection.

Shared Experiences: Creating memories and experiences with your partner further deepens your bond.

Commitment

This is the stage where the couple decides to commit to each other and strive towards building a shared future.

This stage involves:

Decision-Making: At this stage, it's about genuinely valuing each other and nurturing the connection. Take time to listen, share openly, and show that you care through small, meaningful actions. These moments help deepen the bond and create a lasting, heartfelt connection.

Long-Term Planning: They begin to discuss issues of future development, such as living together, marrying, or having children.

Mutual Support: Each of you encourages the other's ambitions and aspirations and is there to help each other deal with difficulties.

This means that commitment is not easy and does not just come as a breeze; it is rewarding and helps make a relationship last.

Thus, it will help you manage the different aspects of relationships and create a good one with your partner. Every stage is superb and complex, and understanding them can improve your relationship story.

Maintaining Love

Maintaining love in a relationship requires effort; it doesn't occur automatically. Here are some key elements that are vital for fostering a healthy and fulfilling relationship.

Communication and Emotional Intelligence

Expressing Needs and Feelings: Stating needs and feelings means sharing what is in your mind, body, and soul with your partner. This practice is important for building a strong, healthy relationship rooted in trust and intimacy. It's very important to communicate your thoughts, feelings, and desires with your partner. This approach helps prevent misunderstandings and fosters trust.

Active listening is a communicative style that involves paying full attention to your partner without interrupting or criticizing them. It entails being gentle, understanding, and replying appropriately. It is said that when you listen to your partner without interruptions and with full focus, you show them respect. Active listening means being able to hear your partner and offer a proper response.

Non-Verbal Communication: Non-verbal communication is the use of gestures and signals in place of words. It includes gestures, eye contact, facial expressions, posture, and tone of voice. These elements are essential in communication and, therefore, in the process of sharing and receiving information. There are instances where language, gestures like eye contact, and tone of voice are used to send messages. Being aware of such a thing can help improve communication and the relationship. This includes gestures, movements, and the general appearance of the body.

For instance, if one folds his arms, this may be a sign of being defensive, while open body language may be an indication of being receptive.

Self-Awareness: It is the understanding of one's feelings, ideas, and activities. It is the state of being conscious of one's feelings, ideas, and behaviors. It includes being mindful of your emotional responses, how these emotional responses work inside you, and how they affect your behavior with other people. The first principle of emotional intelligence is to know your feelings and emotions. That is why when you are aware of your feelings, you can control them rather than respond to them carelessly. Self-awareness enables you to comprehend the effect of your behavior on other people. The first process is to identify the basis for controlling them.

Emotional Regulation: This refers to the ability to appropriately manage and respond to one's emotions. It involves recognizing your feelings, understanding their impact, and controlling your reactions. Being aware of and managing your emotions, especially during conflicts, helps you stay calm and address issues constructively. This approach prevents escalation and promotes problem-solving. It changes your emotional responses to suit the needs of the situation that you are in. When you are able to control your feelings, you will not let the situation get out of hand during a conflict; this is because conflicts tend to escalate when one is too emotional. When emotions are well handled, one is able to think of ways to solve the problem instead of acting unthinkingly. This results in better conflict resolution.

The Importance of Trust and Respect

Reliability and Integrity: Both partners must prove their trustworthiness to gain the other's trust. Being faithful to their word and not deceiving each other strengthens the relationship.

Transparency: Being honest with yourself and others about thoughts, feelings, and actions helps build trust. It means being open with your partner and sharing your life with them so that they do not doubt you. Consistency means always being by your partner's side and doing the same things you have been doing to build trust in the relationship.

Valuing Individuality means accepting your partner for who they are, their assets, ideas, and personal space. It means encouraging them to develop as individuals without intruding on their privacy.

Appreciation and Kindness: It is essential to thank your partner often and treat them well. These relationship actions matter a lot and bring about respect when they feel appreciated.

Support and Encouragement: Supporting the small things related to your partner's goals and dreams are, is one way to show that you value their aspirations. Being a source of encouragement for your partner helps keep the relationship strong.

Cultivating and Maintaining Love

It is, therefore, essential to understand the psychology of love and the stages of a romantic relationship so that one can manage the prospects of love. Here are some practical tips. Here are some valuable tips.

Practice Gratitude: Make it a habit to express appreciation for your partner and your relationship regularly. This positive reinforcement helps deepen the connection and strengthen the bond between them.

Spend Quality Time Together: Make sure you have time for each other, do things together, and develop new experiences. This helps build bonds and fosters intimacy.

Resolve Conflicts Constructively: When handling conflicts, go into problem-solving mode. Do not focus on who did what but on how to solve the issue.

Keep the Romance Alive: Keeping the romance alive is so important. Surprise your partner occasionally, show affection, and find ways to keep the spark burning. A little effort goes a long way in keeping your connection exciting and meaningful.

Thus, incorporating elements such as effective communication, emotional intelligence, trust, and respect into a relationship can build a strong and long-lasting one. This approach affords a solid base for navigating the rough and smooth parts of love.

PART TWO

MARRIAGE

Chapter 4

The Institution of Marriage

Marriage has always been and remains to this day a social construct that has changed and developed over the years. It is a legal and cultural relationship between two people who agree to marry each other, and this marriage confers certain rights and duties on the two, their children, and their respective families. Historically speaking, marriage was more of a way of combining two families with all the necessary concerns of economic, political, and social nature. In many societies, marriage was not based on love, but rather, arrangements were made by the families of the would-be couple. In the present society, the notion of marriage has evolved to be more of a union of two people in love and with high levels of respect. However, there are still cultural variations that define the notion and the practices of marriage across different societies.

Western Cultures

Marriage is often viewed as a personal choice based on romantic love. There is a significant focus on individual rights and equality within the partnership. In Western cultures, marriage is often seen as a personal decision influenced by romantic love and mutual attraction.

In many Western societies, individuals typically choose their own partners based on romantic feelings and personal compatibility. This contrasts with cultures where marriages might be arranged by families or influenced by social and economic considerations. Romantic love is highly valued, and the decision to marry is often based on emotional connection, shared values, and mutual respect. There is a strong emphasis on individual rights within the marriage. Both partners are seen as equals, with equal say in decisions affecting their lives and relationships. Gender equality is a significant aspect, with both partners often sharing responsibilities such as household chores, financial contributions, and parenting duties.

Western cultures typically have legal frameworks that support individual rights within marriage, including laws related to property, divorce, and child custody. These laws aim to protect the interests of both partners, primarily women, and ensure fair treatment. Social norms also support the idea of equality and partnership, encouraging open communication and mutual support in relationships.

Over time, there has been a shift towards more egalitarian relationships, with increasing acceptance of diverse family structures and roles. This includes same-sex marriages, cohabitation without marriage, and blended families. The focus on personal fulfillment and happiness has led to a greater acceptance of divorce if the marriage is no longer satisfying or healthy for either partner. Understanding these aspects helps to appreciate how Westerners view marriage as a partnership based on love, equality, and mutual respect.

Eastern Cultures

In many Asian cultures, marriage is often viewed as a union that extends beyond the couple to include their families. It is a union focused on duty, respect, responsibility, and harmony. Marriage is seen as a way to strengthen familial ties and create alliances between families. This perspective is deeply rooted in traditions and cultural values that emphasize the importance of family and community. The involvement of families in the marriage process helps ensure that the union benefits both parties socially and economically.

Marriages in these cultures often emphasize duty and respect for both families. This includes honoring family traditions, fulfilling familial obligations, and maintaining harmony within the extended family. Harmony is central, with a strong focus on avoiding conflict and ensuring that relationships are balanced and respectful.

Arranged marriages are still common in many regions, such as India, Japan, and China. Arranged marriages generally follow a structured process involving significant family involvement while varying widely across cultures and regions. In these arrangements, families play an essential role in selecting a suitable partner based on factors like social status, education, and family background. While the idea of arranged marriages might seem outdated to some, many couples in these cultures find that love and affection grow over time, nurtured by mutual respect and shared responsibilities.

Cultural practices like ancestor worship and Confucian principles in East Asia highlight the significance of family continuity and respect for elders, which influence marriage customs. In South Asia, religious traditions also significantly shape marriage practices, featuring rituals and ceremonies that reinforce family unions and the sanctity of marriage.

While traditional views on marriage remain strong, there is a growing trend towards more individual choice and love-based marriages, especially in urban areas. Economic development, higher education levels, and changing social norms are contributing to this shift. However, the balance between tradition and modernity varies widely across different regions and communities.

Understanding these cultural nuances helps us appreciate the diverse ways marriage is perceived and practiced around the world.

African Cultures

In most African societies, marriage is a communal rite that involves the couple, their families, and the community. Marriage customs and traditions differ from one culture to another, but most African cultures have one thing in common: the involvement of the community and the extended family in the marriage process. Matchmaking is another function of the elders and other relatives, for they get to ensure that the couple being married is a suitable one culturally and socially. Marriage ceremonies are usually huge, and everyone in the community is generally involved. It is common for them to have lots of customs and traditions that are performed during the wedding, and these involve the whole village.

Some of the customs that are still practiced to this day include the bride price, also known as lobola. It entails the groom's side offering a price for the bride in the form of gifts or money to the bride's side to complete the marriage. This practice shows that the woman and her family are highly valued. The bride's price is the way in which the couple becomes legal, and the groom has to show respect to the bride's family. It also represents the groom's willingness and capacity to sustain his new family.

The payment may be in the form of money, livestock, goods, or a combination of these. For instance, among the Maasai of Kenya and Tanzania, cattle are used as the bride price. The amount of the bride price can differ depending on the bride's family background, education, and many other factors. In some cases, the bride price can be extremely high.

Bride price practices have considerably changed over the years with the help of modern ideas, thus resulting in several changes and developments. High bride prices may cause a tremendous financial burden on the groom and his family, which may result in debt or financial burden. This has led to demand for a more realistic and symbolic amount. In some areas, governments have come in to regulate or put a ceiling on the bride price to avoid exploitive and financial hardships. For instance, Kenya has enacted into law that a symbolic bride price is enough to meet cultural requirements.

The negative aspect of gender equality is that it slams the practice of bride price for buying women and reinforces gender roles. This has caused much controversy and social movements against the practice. As the focus is on women's rights and freedom, changes in the bride price concept and customs are being observed. Some communities are now moving towards new and better ways of marriage that respect women's freedoms and their contributions. In response to modern critiques, some communities are now making the practice less material and more symbolic with a view of giving due respect to tradition without having to spend a lot of money.

It is common to see many couples striving to blend traditional customs with modern values. This can be achieved by agreeing on a bride price that reflects mutual respect as equal partners rather than as a mere business transaction. Some countries have implemented legal measures to mitigate the negative effects of bride prices on women. In 2015, the Ugandan Supreme Court made a landmark decision stating that the bride price cannot be reclaimed after a divorce, simplifying the process for women to leave abusive marriages.

More and more people are becoming aware of the adverse effects of high bride prices, which has led to greater awareness of the whole process. Communities are thus discussing how to adapt traditional beliefs and customs to the present world. These changes indicate a general shift in conventional beliefs and customs to suit present society's concerns about equality, respect, and financial wisdom.

The family helps the couple, especially in the new phase of their lives, by providing support and advice where necessary. Marriage customs and traditions differ from one culture to another, which is why there is a wide range of traditions. For instance, in some Nigerian ethnic groups, the engagement ceremony is a very important function accompanied by local rituals, while the wedding itself may have a religious significance.

To understand the custom of polygamy, one needs to look at history because it has been practiced in many African societies for centuries with reasons ranging from providing food and shelter to orphaned women to increasing the family's workforce. However, polygamy is no more common as social and cultural changes, and the need for more income have influenced the practice. Many African societies have a culture that emphasizes procreation and reproduction of the family name. Marriage is believed to be a way of having children and raising them, which is considered very important for society.

Research indicates that marriage can provide several advantages over being single, especially in aspects like health and longevity. For instance, married individuals generally exhibit better overall health, with studies demonstrating they are less likely to experience strokes, heart attacks, or depression. They also typically possess stronger immune systems and lower levels of stress.

Married individuals typically live longer than their single counterparts. In terms of survival rates and overall well-being, men, in particular, experience significant benefits from marriage. Furthermore, marriage provides a built-in support system that helps individuals manage stress and confront life's challenges more effectively. Additionally, people are more likely to adopt healthier lifestyles, including improved eating habits and reduced risk-taking behaviors.

However, it's important to note that these benefits are often linked to the quality of the marriage. Unhappy or stressful marriages may negate these advantages.

Legal and Social Aspects

Marriage involves not just a commitment between individuals to be lifelong partners, but also a legal contract that includes specific rights and responsibilities. The legal aspects of marriage can encompass the following.

Property Rights: The rules governing the ownership of property in or disposition of property during the marriage and in the event of a divorce.

Inheritance Rights are legal requirements for the transfer of property ownership in the event of the spouse's death.

Parental legal obligations and rights relating to the nurturing and development of children are beneficial rights for parents when raising children.

In addition, union marriage is usually recognized and accepted by society and is, therefore, considered a significant event in an individual's life. It can also affect one's social rank and determine an individual's role in society.

Common Issues and Challenges in Marriage

Every marriage has problems, and it is easier to solve some of the most common ones by knowing some of the most common ones.

Communication Problems

Definition: Communication problems involve challenges in expressing thoughts, emotions, and desires.

Importance: Poor communication can lead to misunderstandings, anger, and even fights. Good communication is, therefore, vital for tackling any problems that may arise and building a strong relationship.

Financial Stress

Definition: Disagreements about money management, spending, and saving. These conflicts occur when partners are not on the same page regarding financial matters, such as planning a budget and how money is generally spent. This sets the stage for saving and tackling debt.

Importance: Financial stress can significantly strain a marriage. It often symbolizes deeper issues, such as power struggles or differing values.

Financial stress is important because it is one of the biggest causes of arguments in marriages. This, in turn, indicates other issues, including relations, values, and expression. For example, one partner may prefer to spend while the other is a saver, resulting in constant argument and discomfort.

Debt issues can cause anxiety and frequent distress in the relationship, especially when it is one-sided spending. When one of the partners incurs huge expenses without the knowledge of the other, this leads to the development of feelings such as disrespect and financial unbalance.

Emotional Distance: If intimacy is lacking, the couple may feel isolated and alone.

Decreased Satisfaction: The lack of physical and emotional contact can result in disappointment and annoyance in the relationship.

Increased Conflict: When issues are left unresolved, they tend to escalate over time, leading to more frequent disagreements and arguments within the relationship. This can create a cycle of ongoing tension and misunderstanding.

Intimacy Issues

Definition: Concerns with intimacy in marriage consist of problems that affect the aspect of intimacy between the partners. This includes sexual issues such as differences in libido or other preferences and lack of emotional intimacy where the partners are not close.

Importance: Intimacy is a significant factor in building a strong marital relationship. It enhances the feelings of closeness, trust, and satisfaction of the two partners. When intimacy issues are raised, they may cause feelings of isolation, annoyance, and unhappiness, which can negatively impact the relationship.

Sexual Differences: The differences in sexual desires, needs, or expectations within a relationship can sometimes lead to misunderstandings and, consequently, discomfort. For instance, if one partner has a higher sex drive than the other, it may result in tension or feelings of rejection. Open communication and mutual understanding are crucial for navigating these differences and maintaining a healthy connection.

Lack of Emotional Connection: Emotional intimacy refers to sharing feelings, ideas, and stories. When partners fail to communicate effectively, they may not share the same feelings, which can result in a lack of support and comprehension.

Stress and Fatigue: Work, family, or other life demands can cause a lot of stress, which can cut down on the time and energy that could be used for intimacy. This can make emotional and physical intimacy something that one has to do rather than something that is enjoyable.

Medical and Psychological Issues: Some of the disorders that may affect sexual and emotional intimacy include depression, anxiety, or physical illnesses. For instance, erectile dysfunction or low libido can cause stress and, therefore, reduce physical contact.

Effects of Intimacy Issues

Emotional Distance means that if the partners do not engage in emotional and physical intimacy frequently, they will feel alone, which can weaken their bond.

Decreased Satisfaction: However, lack of intimacy results in dissatisfaction and annoyance, hence making the partners feel unappreciated in the relationship.

Increased Conflict: Unresolved intimacy problems can lead to frequent fights and resentment, which can worsen the relationship.

Addressing Intimacy Issues

Open Communication: Expressing one's needs, wants, and problems can help people in a relationship comprehend each other and agree to a certain extent.

Professional Help: Sometimes, seeking the services of a therapist or counselor can be beneficial for resolving intimacy issues and improving relationships.

Making Time for Each Other: It's crucial to spend quality time together, especially when both of you have busy schedules, to strengthen your emotional and physical bond.

Infidelity Issues

Definition: Infidelity refers to cheating, which includes emotional, physical, and digital cheating. Most common affairs start with the development of a close relationship between one spouse and another person. This relationship grows with emotions. Most infidelity is not always physical affairs, but overall, it can be very destructive as it goes a long way in eroding the trust and the emotional security that is supposed to be enjoyed in a marriage. It results in feelings of betrayal, anger, and sadness, which can take a while to heal from. Infidelity is very painful because it targets the most essential elements of a relationship, which include trust and respect.

Infidelity can deeply impact the foundation of trust and emotional connection in a relationship. Whether stemming from unmet needs, lack of communication, or other underlying factors, it frequently results in feelings of betrayal, guilt, and resentment. Addressing infidelity necessitates open dialogue, accountability, and a willingness to rebuild trust. Let's explore how infidelity can create challenges and ways to navigate its effects within relationships.

Parenting Differences

Definition: This can include differing opinions on parenting, including discipline and the balancing of roles.

Importance: I believe that strong and stable parenting significantly contributes to creating a positive family environment. Addressing differences ensures that parents are aligned, ultimately benefiting the children.

Work-Life Balance

Work-life balance refers to the harmony between professional responsibilities and personal life. It involves the ability to manage work commitments alongside other aspects of life, such as family, leisure, and health, in a manner that fosters a balanced and healthy lifestyle.

Theoretical Underpinning and Practices

Time Management: Allocations of adequate time for work and for other personal needs and activities in order that the person does not become burnt out and is still productive.

Boundary Setting: Setting some rules to define what works and what does not to ensure that one does not cross the line.

Flexibility: The opportunity to change the work timings in accordance with personal needs and requirements and vice versa.

Prioritization: Understanding and undertaking tasks and activities that are significant in the workplace and in the rest of one's life.

Importance of Work-Life Balance

Mental Health: It also helps reduce and enhance stress and prevent mental burnout.

Physical Health: Makes people practice healthy living because it allows for work, sleep, and fun.

Relationships: Enhances the bonds of relationships by allowing enough time to be spent with family and friends.

Job Satisfaction: Enhances job satisfaction and worker output since it avoids overwork and creates a healthy work culture.

Therefore, it is essential to be able to balance work and the rest of one's life for a healthy life and better long-term results.

Chapter 5

Strategies for

Overcoming Challenges

It is possible to overcome obstacles if one puts effort and dedication into the relationship. Some strategies include: Some strategies include:

Seeking Professional Help: Marriage counseling is always a good idea. It creates a safe environment for both parties to discuss problems and work on improving communication.

Prioritizing the Relationship: It's essential to spend quality time together, to be thankful for each other, and to keep the flame alive in the relationship.

Developing Resilience: It is crucial for couples to have the emotional strength to deal with the positive and negative aspects of marriage. This includes having a positive attitude, being there for your partner, and growing in the process.

Real-Life Examples of Strong Marriages

John and Emily

John and Emily have been married for thirty years, and they still love each other, as they did the first day they met. The couple has revealed that the reason behind their happy marriage is the respect they have for each other as well as having to open up to each other. The couple has a schedule where they have weekly 'date nights' to spend time with each other and also share how they feel and what they plan to do in life. In every challenge that they encounter, they solve it as a family and in a way that will be favorable to both of them.

Raj and Priya

Raj and Priya live in India, and their parents have arranged their marriage. At the beginning of their relationship, the couple did not share many common aspects, but they were able to develop a strong relationship based on the values of patience and understanding since they had a lot in common. The couple has a lot of respect for each other's culture and has been able to mix the two cultures and the traditions of both families. These are happy marriages because the couples have one thing in common: the desire to take care of each other and their families.

Kota and Teruko

Kota and Teruko live in Japan and have been married for 20 years. Both of them know the value of individuality and personal freedom, as well as the value of one's passion and dreams. As for conflict-solving strategies, they tend to reason about the problem and come up with a solution. They are both historically strong, and in their perspective, beliefs communicate and uphold, and family solves conflicts and community. To understand and solve the concept problems that may occur in marriage using effective strategies seems to be helpful in building a strong and happy marriage. This part of the book is intended to help you understand the aspects of married life as well as arming you with the information and skills that are necessary to build a happy married life.

The Role of Spirituality in Marriage

Spirituality can significantly enhance and support a marital relationship. It fosters a deeper bond between spouses, nurturing a sense of direction, purpose, unity, and resilience. However, spirituality can have an immense impact on marriage:

Spirituality is the belief in the existence of the soul, the spirit, and the afterlife, and it often involves the concept of the interconnectedness of all things, which means that in spirituality, everything is connected. Therefore, in spirituality, a person is not isolated, but rather, they are part of a larger whole that includes others, the environment, and the spiritual realm. In relationships, it means that spouses are one with each other, and this oneness strengthens the bond between them. When couples share spiritual beliefs and practices, they build a common platform of tolerance and appreciation. This shared spiritual path can improve their affection and physical contact and, therefore, enrich their relationship.

> *"A successful marriage requires falling in love many times, always with the same person."*
> — *Mignon McLaughlin.*

Spirituality can help couples find a purpose in their lives other than the two of them. In many cultures and spiritual traditions, marriage is considered a sacred bond in which each person has a role to play in achieving specific goals or for the purpose of procreation and raising God-fearing children. This has been seen to help couples by giving them something to fall back on when either of them is faced with a challenge.

> *"Marriage is not just spiritual communion, it is also remembering to take out the trash."*
> — *Joyce Brothers.*

Enhancing Resilience

Religion and other spiritual beliefs and practices help couples find something to hold on to in times of stress and difficulty. Some beneficial activities include praying, meditating, and attending church. Spirituality also promotes forgiveness and compassion, which are important in resolving conflicts and healing emotional wounds.

"A strong marriage requires two people who choose to love each other even on those days when they struggle to like each other."
— *Dave Willis.*

Encouraging Personal Growth

Marriage is a powerful tool that fosters personal growth and spirituality. Throughout married life, spouses can discover their capabilities and limitations, giving them an opportunity to grow as individuals. It is a relationship between two people that promotes individual development and strengthens their bond.

"Marriage is the highest state of friendship. If happy, it lessens our cares by dividing them, at the same time that it doubles our pleasures by mutual participation."
— *Samuel Richardson.*

Building a Supportive Community

Spiritual communities are also beneficial in that they can be a source of strength for married couples. Having a network of people who share the same or similar ideas and beliefs as the couple can encourage, support, and even guide them. This feeling of being part of something larger helps solidify the bond between the couple and their devotion to faith.

> *"Great marriages are contagious. If you want one, surround yourself with couples who have one."*
> — *Anonymous.*

Real-Life Examples of Spirituality in Marriage
Dave and Paula

In an interview with Dave and Paula, the American couple stated that they have a habit of regularly praying together every day, attending church services, and hanging out with friends in the congregation frequently. Their faith has given them a reason and a way of looking at life and facing problems with kindness and time. Religion gives them meaning in life and is their source of strength to deal with difficulties in a calm and kind manner.

Anil and Meera

Anil and Meera, a couple from India, embrace Hindu spirituality as a significant part of their lives. They strengthen their relationship and uphold their cultural values by participating in religious festivals and rituals. This shared spiritual practice helps them stay connected and support each other through any challenges.

Kenji and Aiko

Kenji and Aiko, from Japan, practice Zen Buddhism in their marriage. They both meditate and adhere to the principle of mindfulness, which enables them to be present and fully appreciate each moment. They embrace their differing beliefs, which has fostered peace and harmony in their relationship.

Faith is crucial in a relationship. It can strengthen the bond between couples and provide them with vital moral support to face any hardship. Consequently, spirituality is equally important. It helps couples deepen their connection, overcome challenges together, and cultivate greater happiness in their shared lives.

Relationships, much like waves, are ever-changing and dynamic. They experience highs and lows, moments of calm, and times of turbulence. With patience, trust, and a commitment to growth, couples can navigate these shifts, finding balance and harmony. Embrace the journey, understanding that every challenge deepens the connection and moves your partnership forward.

Marriage involves showing up each day and choosing the life you're creating together with your spouse. Challenges will arise, and your spouse may not always fulfill every expectation. Concentrate on what works, nurture it with gratitude, and accept imperfection. Each challenge presents an opportunity to grow closer, strengthen your bond, and rediscover the reasons you chose each other. With love, patience, and effort, your relationship can become truly remarkable.

PART THREE

DIVORCE

Chapter 6

Embracing Healing

Divorce is one of the most significant decisions a person can make in their lifetime, and it is a process filled with numerous emotions, struggles, and consequences. This book provides a real-world perspective on what divorce entails, how one can cope with it, and how to start anew after a divorce. Divorce can evoke a range of emotions, such as sadness, anger, relief, and confusion. These feelings can be intense and may fluctuate over time, depending on the stage of the divorce. Emotional trauma often stems from the disruption of a close relationship, changes in daily routines, and the uncertainty of the future.

First, it is important to know that people react to divorce in rather different ways. Some may even feel free, while others may feel sad or guilty. These feelings are normal, and one should be allowed to go through the process of healing. It is very helpful to have someone to listen to and encourage you during this period of change, and therefore, it is advisable to seek the support of friends, family, or a professional counselor when going through this divorce process.

Divorce is unavoidable, and therefore, it is a process that must be confronted. This is due to the emotional, legal, psychological, and physical challenges that divorce entails. These obstacles can be overcome by understanding the necessary steps, developing effective strategies, and maintaining a positive attitude to create a joyful life once again. It is important to recognize that divorce does not necessarily equate to starting anew; with time and self-care, one can emerge as a better person.

The Good, the Bad and the Ugly

Divorce can be viewed from different angles. To some, it is a way to liberation and happiness. To others, it is a time of sorrow and financial burden. Knowing that divorce is not black and white can be helpful when going through this challenging process.

The Good: A marriage breakup can offer a new beginning, allowing people to leave toxic or violent relationships, enjoy their lives, and develop themselves further.

The Bad: Divorce can evoke many emotions, such as loss, anger, and sadness. It can also change the structure of a family and impact children.

The Ugly: Divorce laws in the United States and many Western countries create significant financial challenges, with men often bearing the brunt. Legal fees, alimony, child support, and asset division can significantly affect financial stability, transforming divorce into both an emotional and economic struggle.

Understanding Divorce

Divorce can leave a gap in one's life where a person loses a spouse and the dreams and aspirations that were held for the future. This can lead to feelings of loss, grief, and other emotional disorders. The psychological stress of divorce can also result in additional psychological problems such as anxiety, depression, substance abuse, and more. It is important to recognize these issues to find their solutions

Divorce can shake one's identity, especially when a person has defined their role in life by their marital status. This situation can cause stress and uncertainty, leading individuals to seek their identity. The loss of friends and other sources of support can create feelings of isolation and loneliness. Therefore, it is important to consider financial planning during the rebuilding process, which includes reviewing the couple's budget and social network as part of healing. Furthermore, some areas involve understanding one's rights and obligations. Some of the costs incurred during the divorce process include attorney fees, court fees, and other expenses such as alimony or child support.

Legal Processes and Implications

Filing for divorce is the initial legal step indicating that a marriage is nearing its end. Divorce laws vary by state, and one must typically follow several processes.

Filing for Divorce: The first party involved is the petitioner, who goes to court with a petition for divorce and the reasons for seeking it. The spouse initiating the divorce is referred to as the petitioner. This individual appears in court and completes documents such as a divorce petition or a complaint within a particular jurisdiction.

The petition provides essential information about both spouses, including their names and addresses, as well as the dates and locations of their marriage. The petitioner must put forth the reasons for seeking a divorce. These reasons may differ from state to state but can generally fall under categories such as irreconcilable differences, adultery, abandonment, or cruelty, amongst others. The petition specifies what the petitioner requests from the divorce: child custody, spousal support or alimony, property division, and any other necessary considerations.

The petitioner presents the divorce petition to the concerned court, which is then signed and filed in the county court. Some local rules may apply, and specific periods of residence in the jurisdiction may have to be met.

Following this, the petitioner has to file the divorce papers with the other spouse, the respondent. This involves giving the respondent a copy of the petition and a summons to appear in court. According to the local rules, service can be made by a professional process server, a sheriff, or, in some cases, mail. The petitioner cannot give the respondent the papers directly, which may lead to controversies.

The husband and wife have a specific time (usually 20-30 days) to respond to the petition. Their response can follow the terms set out by the petitioner or contradict them.

If the respondent fails to respond within the set time, the court may enter a default judgment in favor of the petitioner. This means that the divorce is granted as petitioned by the petitioner. In the case of divorce, both parties may have attorneys to represent them. An attorney can help ensure that they get a fair hearing. Divorce is a formal legal procedure that allows both sides of a case to state their case and come up with a reasonable decision.

Divorce has consequences and can significantly impact a person's finances. Most men will have to pay child support and alimony and divide their marital assets. Attorney fees and other legal expenses can accumulate quickly, making divorce costly.

Divorce can lead to several feelings, including loss, anger, guilt, and a sense of freedom. It is common to feel a sense of loss and uncertainty about the future. Divorce can have serious psychological effects, such as declining self-esteem, mental health issues, and diminished quality of life. These feelings deserve recognition, and seeking help from professionals is advisable to address these challenges.

Strategies for Emotional Healing

Divorce is a significant loss, and one should be allowed to mourn. You should admit that you feel unhappy, offended, or even perplexed. Sometimes, it may help to talk to a therapist or a counselor who can help a person deal with their emotions and develop ways of handling them. A mental health professional can assist you in dealing with the psychological impact of divorce. Therefore, taking care of your physical and mental health is vital. Exercise regularly, have a proper diet, sleep for enough time, and do things that may make you happy and relaxed.

You can also depend on your friends and family, who are always there for you. Sharing your feelings with them is essential, as they typically listen and support you. It is important to be around people facing similar challenges, as this can be quite encouraging. It is comforting, to say the least, to be among those who understand what you are going through firsthand. Additionally, it is essential to know your legal rights and options.

Seeking advice from a divorce lawyer can be beneficial to address legal matters and ensure you are well protected. A financial advisor can assist in managing the economic effects of divorce, helping with budgeting, property division, and future planning.

Rebuilding and Moving Forward

It is important to note that life after divorce can be quite complex yet very fulfilling. It's essential to look toward the future and set personal and career-related goals. This approach provides a sense of direction and purpose while rebuilding your life. This period of divorce also brings numerous changes, which should be embraced as opportunities for growth and self-discovery.

The following are some of the helpful tips for coming up with new routines. It is advisable to look for things that can be done and that will be helpful in the process of healing. If you have children, then the well-being of the children should be your number one concern. Both of you need to develop a co-parenting plan that will help you both be good parents to your children and give them the necessary care. It is also essential to ensure that you keep on having a good and healthy relationship with your ex-spouse.

This can help reduce conflict and ensure a favorable co-parenting environment. If you have none, it's essential to work on building good relationships with friends, family, and other partners. It's also advisable to surround yourself with people who will positively influence you and be there for you.

Divorce is one of the most challenging and bitter experiences in any marriage, yet it also presents an opportunity to start a new chapter in one's life. Understanding the legal and emotional sides of divorce, along with the facts, can help you face the process with strength. This knowledge makes it easier to cope, start healing, and take the first steps toward rebuilding your life.

Chapter 7

Is Marriage Still a Good Option

In today's fast-paced world, marriage has undergone transformations. The impact of technology and the widespread use of social media have shaped our ways of communication, relationship-building, and social interactions. Despite these changes, marriage continues to be important and valuable in society, with many considering it a treasured tradition. Here are some factors to consider when deciding whether to get married.

People marry for various reasons, including love, companionship, procreation, and the legitimacy of children. Marriage formalizes a strong commitment, providing stability and security within a relationship. It establishes a solid foundation for raising children and offers a support system for facing life's challenges together. Furthermore, marriage is a universal tradition that strengthens social bonds and fosters a sense of connection and belonging within a community.

Marriage enhances the emotional and physical closeness between partners. It represents the union of two individuals, which helps strengthen their emotional connection and sexual intimacy. Furthermore, marriage offers opportunities for shared experiences, support, and friendship that contribute to the well-being of both individuals involved.

It is important for people to have someone to turn to, especially in times of hardship. A happy marriage relies on communication and cooperation. Therefore, marriage can come with its fair share of duties, obligations, and conflicts that need to be resolved. It is important to encourage accountability, which is a process through which both partners can develop individually as well as together as a couple. This can also help improve the communication between them.

However, being married does come with its difficulties and considerations. It entails dedicating time, effort, and money. Both partners may need to make compromises. Effective communication, mutual understanding, and nurturing the relationship are essential for a marriage to thrive. Furthermore, the expectations and pressures from society regarding marriage can occasionally create tension or disagreements within a partnership

When considering marriage, take a step back and evaluate your relationship with your partner. Marriage demands a deep bond, understanding, and love. Effective communication, mutual trust, and shared values are vital for establishing a strong foundation for a lasting commitment. If you both genuinely feel connected, supportive, and respectful towards each other, marriage could be the next natural step in your relationship.

Considering your lifestyle and long-term aspirations is essential when contemplating marriage, as they can affect your freedom of choice in career and financial stability. Talking about your future goals, such as buying a home, starting a family, or advancing in your career, can help you determine whether marriage fits into your plans. It is important for any couple to balance personal and shared goals in order to lead a happy life.

Furthermore, marriage has some legal consequences that everyone needs to know before jumping into it. Issues such as property ownership, financial responsibilities, and legal decision-making (e.g., healthcare directives) require consideration. It's important to seek legal advice or consult with a family lawyer to ensure you understand the legal implications of marriage and how it will affect your rights and obligations.

Personal Values and Goals

Marriage is a strong foundation on which couples can create their families, share common objectives, and even have children. Marriage might be the best choice if you appreciate the value of having a life partner, commitment, and being with someone for the long run.

Emotional and Financial Stability

Marriage can be a great source of support and financial stability, offering a partnership where you share responsibilities and tackle life's challenges together. However, it's important to have open conversations about your financial goals and align on priorities, and expectations. Being on the same page helps create trust, avoid misunderstandings, and set you up for a harmonious future. Remember, a successful marriage isn't just about shared finances, it's about working as a team to achieve the life you both envision.

Marriage is a legal institution offering numerous advantages, including tax benefits, property rights, important medical decisions, and different forms of social acceptance. These benefits can promote confidence and a sense of freedom.

Communication and Compatibility

Effective relationship management involves proper communication and compatibility in the modern world. Technology can play a significant role in developing relationships but, at the same time, can bring problems as well. Thus, it is important to apply digital tools in the proper manner to improve communication and relationships rather than to deteriorate it.

A strong marriage is built on compromise and adaptability. Couples need to grow in a fast-changing world shaped by technology and innovation. This means both partners should be open to new ways of communicating and supporting each other to stay connected and strengthen their relationship, no matter what life brings.

Good communication is at the heart of any strong relationship. As the saying goes, *"Communication is the key to a happy home."* Take the time to listen to each other and express your thoughts and needs openly. When challenges come up, approach them together as a team. Open dialogue builds trust, deepens understanding, and creates a space where both partners feel valued and heard. Strengthening your communication skills establishes the foundation for a healthy and fulfilling relationship.

Reflecting on the Journey: Lessons Learned and Personal Growth

The term love has evolved over time, shaped by the historical and cultural contexts of each era. In the past, love was often intertwined with tradition. Parents played a central role in selecting partners for their children, guided by societal norms such as matching social status before arranging marriages. As we have explored the themes of love, marriage, and divorce more deeply, we can draw key conclusions about their processes and impacts.

Self-awareness is the process of gaining a deeper understanding of oneself and one's personal identity. It allows one to initiate action or choose not to, all while having a reason to live. Self-awareness is crucial for fostering positive interpersonal relationships, allowing individuals to articulate their ideas more accurately and make appropriate decisions.

Resilience: I think it is very important to be resilient in any relationship, and that is why it is important to work on it. Your ability to deal with emotional problems and any strength that may occur is imperative. Resilience enables one to face the issues and, in the long run, grow to be a better person.

Communication: I believe that communication is one of the most important factors in building and maintaining a successful relationship. Skills like active listening, honesty, telling it as it is, and striving for personal growth are essential. Practicing these builds trust, fosters understanding, and creates a deeper, more meaningful connection with your partner. It's not about perfection but showing up, being authentic, and growing together.

Growth: Every relationship should be a source of growth. Consider using every experience gained to improve the relationship and the individuals involved. Consider these tips for nurturing and fostering meaningful relationships.

Prioritize Building Connections: Nurture your relationships by dedicating time to meaningful experiences with your partner and loved ones. Spending quality time together and creating lasting memories enhances emotional bonds and solidifies your connection.

Embrace Change: This involves being flexible to meet future challenges. It will also assist you in handling another element that should be considered as relationships change.

Practice Empathy: It is important to support your partner's acceptance of change and to address their needs with sensitivity. An important process that occurs is the empathetic transformation, as it fosters growth in relationships. Treat them at a personal level and help them in their change

Set Boundaries: To sustain a relationship, it is important to establish boundaries, communicate your needs, and respect your partner's boundaries.

Seek Support: If you ever need help, it is okay to reach out to people. You can seek therapy, talk to friends, or even join support groups. Having people around who you can rely on is very important and helpful. It is nice to have people to interact with to enhance one's happiness, but it is also crucial to understand that relationships are not without their difficulties. Here are some common struggles faced by partners.

Communication Problems

Misunderstandings: Misunderstandings frequently occur when communication is vague or ineffective. These gaps can result in confusion and conflicts between individuals, generating unnecessary tension and impairing relationships.

Lack of Active Listening: Failing to pay attention when your partner is speaking can make them feel as though their thoughts and feelings are dismissed or unimportant.

Avoidance: Avoiding difficult conversations or avoiding addressing issues can worsen problems over time. This approach often exacerbates tensions and leads to a more strained and disconnected relationship. Open communication is essential for resolving underlying concerns and fostering understanding.

Trust Issues

Trust issues can place significant strain on a relationship, making it challenging for both partners to feel secure and connected. These difficulties often stem from past experiences where trust was violated—such as infidelity, dishonesty, or emotional neglect. The pain from previous betrayals, broken promises, or controlling behavior can have a lasting effect, complicating one's ability to fully trust their partner again.

If you're in a relationship and facing trust issues, it's important to approach the situation with patience and empathy. Take time to communicate openly with your partner about your feelings and concerns without placing blame. Rebuilding trust requires effort from both sides—it may involve being more transparent, demonstrating consistency, and creating a safe space where you both feel heard and supported. Healing isn't easy, but with mutual commitment and understanding, it's possible to move forward and strengthen your bond. Remember, trust grows when both partners work together to nurture honesty and respect.

Signs of Trust Issues

Constant Suspicion: When one partner consistently questions the actions and intentions of the other without valid evidence or justification, it can create an atmosphere of mistrust. This behavior often leads to excessive questioning, frequent interrogations, and an escalating sense of discomfort or unease within the relationship.

Jealousy: Experiencing envy over your partner's interactions with others—such as friends, coworkers, or family members—can foster feelings of insecurity. This may result in attempts to control or limit their relationships, which can create tension and strain within the partnership. Open communication and trust are vital to addressing these feelings constructively.

Checking Behaviors: Engaging in actions like checking your partner's phone, internet browsing history, emails, or social media accounts without their consent is a violation of privacy. Such behavior can significantly damage trust and create tension in the relationship, making open and honest communication even more essential.

Overreacting to Small Issues: Exaggerating problems and jumping to negative conclusions in situations that don't warrant it can lead to unnecessary stress and disagreements.

Emotional Distance Issue: In some relationship dynamics, one or both partners may begin to distance themselves as a way to avoid vulnerability and intimacy – acting as a protective measure against the pain of getting hurt.

Impact on the Relationship

Suspicion is one factor that results in arguments and conflicts, which mainly involve faithfulness and truthfulness. Such conflicts can be frequent and become a pattern of the relationship with no resolution. The emotional distance caused by trust issues can make or break a relationship. It hinders the partners from feeling intimacy and affection, thus preventing them from fostering closeness and support.

Trust problems may also trigger feelings of insecurity and a lack of self-confidence in a relationship, making either partner feel inadequate or constantly anxious about abandonment or betrayal by the other person.

Rebuilding Trust

Effective Communication is Key: This means that communication should always be clear and truthful in order to maintain a relationship or partnership. Both partners need to share how they feel, what they are thinking, and what they want. The partner who has been cheated on or experienced betrayal must be able to express their feelings, and the other partner should listen to understand what concerns he or she has.

Seeking Professional Help: Considering couples therapy or counselling can create a space for working through trust-related struggles with the guidance of a trained therapist. This professional support can help both individuals better manage their feelings and enhance their communication skills while developing effective strategies to restore trust within the relationship dynamics. Similarly, therapy sessions can help to identify other issues that could have led to the breach of trust in the relationship.

Establishing Rules: Another important aspect is rebuilding trust in a relationship. The couple must define rules for the new coexistence, and both partners must decide what specific actions are permitted and which are prohibited.

This may involve creating guidelines for communication, interaction, and transparency guidelines regarding daily routines. By respecting and maintaining these boundaries, partners can create a sense of safety and security.

Patience and Time: Reestablishing trust requires patience and time, as healing is a journey with setbacks for both individuals involved in the relationship. Therefore, it is essential for couples to remain committed and communicate effectively to navigate trust issues and strengthen their bond.

Building trust in a relationship is not always straightforward, which is why it is considered an art. Nevertheless, with the support of each other, genuine and ongoing conversations, and professional guidance, it is possible to tackle these challenges and foster a healthier type of connection.

Financial Stress

Differences in attitudes toward money can cause tension in a relationship, especially when partners have conflicting spending habits. These financial disagreements can strain communication and result in misunderstandings, highlighting the importance of aligning financial goals and priorities.

Debt: Financial burdens, such as debt, can lead to stress and conflict. Budgeting: Managing money can sometimes lead to disputes when individuals disagree on budgeting and managing their finances.

Intimacy Issues

Physical Intimacy: Physical intimacy is an important part of feeling close and connected in a relationship. Challenges, like mismatched levels of desire or struggles with physical closeness, can create emotional distance between partners. The key to overcoming this is open and honest communication—talking about these feelings with kindness and understanding. You can strengthen your connection and build a deeper bond by addressing these issues with empathy.

Emotional Intimacy: When a relationship lacks emotional intimacy, both partners can feel alone, unappreciated, or even unloved. Emotional intimacy is about feeling deeply connected, understood, and supported by your partner. To build this connection, it's important to share your thoughts and feelings openly and create a space where trust can grow. When nurtured, emotional intimacy strengthens your bond and helps both of you feel valued and loved.

Life Changes

Life changes, such as career shifts, parenting responsibilities, and health issues, often challenge relationships. These changes can introduce stress and alter dynamics. Let's explore how these challenges affect relationships.

Career Transitions

Changes in a career, such as job loss, a shift in focus, or the pursuit of new professional goals, can disrupt the balance of a relationship. Financial instability from unemployment or the challenges of adjusting to a new job may create stress. For instance, a partner's late work hours in a new position might lead to feelings of neglect, while differing ambitions could result in misalignment.

Parenting Challenges

Parenting often entails significant emotional and logistical pressures. Conflicts can emerge from differing parenting philosophies, such as disagreements over discipline or educational choices. Stress from sleepless nights, managing a child's special needs, or balancing responsibilities can lead to communication breakdowns. For example, one parent may feel overwhelmed if the other appears less involved, potentially causing resentment.

Health Concerns: Chronic illnesses or unexpected health issues can strain relationships because they often require lifestyle adjustments, caregiving responsibilities, and emotional support. These changes may lead to feelings of frustration, guilt, or helplessness for both partners. For instance, if one partner's medical condition limits their ability to engage in shared activities, the other may feel isolated or unappreciated. Additionally, managing medical appointments, expenses, or caregiving tasks can alter the relationship dynamics.

Conflict Resolution

Unresolved Conflicts: Avoiding problems can lead to lingering feelings among partners involved in a conflict situation. When handling disagreements or disputes, some individuals avoid confrontation, while others address the issues, which may sometimes lead to conflicts.

Escalation: Letting disagreements grow without reaching a resolution can harm the relationship

Time Management

Effective time management is crucial for nurturing strong and healthy relationships. The demands of work, family, and personal responsibilities often pull us in various directions, leaving little space for connection. When busy schedules take over, intentionally setting aside time for loved ones becomes increasingly difficult. However, by acknowledging the significance of time management, you can take proactive measures to strengthen your bond.

Let's explore two key areas, busy schedules and quality time, to understand their impact on relationships and how to address these challenges.

Busy Schedules: Life's many commitments, such as work obligations, caregiving responsibilities, and personal goals, can feel overwhelming. Balancing all these aspects often leaves limited time and energy for meaningful connection. When schedules are packed, it's common for relationships to feel strained due to a lack of attention. Here are some practical tips.

- Set clear priorities for tasks and responsibilities.

- Use a shared calendar to plan time for both individual and relationship-focused activities.

- Break down tasks into manageable chunks to reduce stress and free up time for connection.

Quality Time: Spending quality time with your partner is essential for nurturing intimacy, trust, and emotional connection. Without it, relationships can weaken over time as communication declines. Quality time isn't merely about the quantity—it's about being fully present and engaged during shared moments. Here are some practical tips.

- Plan regular date nights or share time on hobbies together.

- Disconnect from technology during these times to maintain focus on your partner.

- Celebrate small victories or milestones together to create lasting memories.

Compatibility Issues:

Compatibility challenges are a natural part of any relationship and can serve as a pathway to growth and understanding. Instead of seeing them as obstacles, view them as opportunities to strengthen your bond. Couples can navigate challenges through mutual respect and care by embracing differences and communicating openly.

Focus on what unites you: shared values, dreams, and goals, while also appreciating each other's unique qualities. Love isn't about finding a perfect match; it's about building a partnership grounded in patience, empathy, and adaptability. By choosing to grow together and support one another through life's ups and downs, challenges can transform into the foundation for an even stronger relationship.

Conflicting core values or different life goals can create tension in a relationship, as these foundational differences may cause friction. Furthermore, lifestyle choices—such as varying social habits, hobbies, or daily routines—can lead to disagreements. Recognizing and addressing these differences with understanding and open communication is essential for promoting harmony and mutual respect.

External Influences

Influence from family and friends, or their absence of support, can profoundly impact a relationship. These outside factors may create stress, misunderstandings, or a feeling of imbalance, highlighting the importance for partners to communicate and establish boundaries to safeguard their connection.

Social Media: Misusing social media or comparing your relationship to others displayed online can create unrealistic expectations. This may lead to dissatisfaction, misunderstandings, and pressure to conform to idealized portrayals, affecting the authenticity of your connection.

Personal Growth

Individual Changes: As people grow and evolve over time, their interests, priorities, or perspectives may shift. If both partners do not adapt to these changes together, they may experience emotional distance and a sense of drifting apart. Open communication and mutual effort are key to maintaining a strong connection as individuals change.

Self-Esteem: Minimizing factors that negatively affect partners' communication during conversations, practicing good manners, and actively seeking input on self-esteem can enhance respect in every relationship. Every relationship encounters unique challenges, and addressing these issues can improve couples' connections. It's essential to manage insecurities and seek assistance from a trusted therapist or counselor, particularly during tough times. This collaboration can be crucial for effectively navigating difficulties.

How can couples improve Trust Issues

Improving your communication skills can greatly enhance your relationships and interactions with others. Here are some tips for becoming a more effective communicator.

Active Listening

Pay Attention: Concentrate on the speaker and avoid distractions, such as your phone, television, or other responsibilities.

To demonstrate that you're listening, use nonverbal cues such as nodding, maintaining eye contact, and leaning slightly forward.

Reflect and Clarify: Restate what the speaker has conveyed to confirm your understanding and pose clarifying questions if necessary.

Be Concise: Get straight to the point without unnecessary details

Use "I" statements: Share your feelings and thoughts with "I" statements to prevent sounding accusatory (e.g., "I feel..." instead of "You always..."). Stay on topic: Focus on the matter at hand to prevent confusion.

Non-Verbal Communication

Body Language: Being aware of nonverbal cues is crucial since they effectively communicate emotions and intentions. Paying attention to body language ensures that your message is consistent and clearly understood by others.

Facial Expressions: Make sure your facial expressions align with your words to avoid sending mixed signals or confusing your partner's understanding. This alignment fosters effective communication and improves clarity in interactions.

Tonality: The tone should align with the message you want to convey, whether it is calm, enthusiastic, or serious. Show empathy and understanding.

Put Yourself in Their Shoes. Try to understand the speaker's perspective and emotions. Empathy allows you to connect on a deeper level, fostering mutual understanding and stronger relationships.

Acknowledge Emotions: Recognize the speaker's feelings and show that you understand their perspective.

Encourage Dialogue: Ask questions that necessitate more than a yes or no response to foster deeper conversations (for example, "How did that make you feel?" instead of "Did you like it?")

Manage Your Emotions

Stay Calm: Regulate your feelings, especially when in a conflict-of-interest situation or when engaged in a contentious discussion.

Take a Break if Needed: If you feel overwhelmed, you can pause the conversation and return to it at a later time.

Be Respectful. Respect involves recognizing, understanding, and valuing the feelings, beliefs, and traditions of others. Demonstrating respect is essential for building strong relationships and fostering a positive, inclusive culture.

Avoid Interrupting: Allow the speaker to finish expressing their thoughts before you respond. It's important to show respect by refraining from interruptions during conversations. Wait until they have shared all their ideas before offering your own opinions.

Respect Differences: Acknowledge and respect differing opinions and perspectives.

Provide Constructive Feedback: Offer specific, actionable feedback that is focused on behavior rather than character. Accept the input provided gracefully, viewing it as a chance for personal growth. Specific and actionable feedback helps individuals understand precisely what they need to improve. Vague feedback can be unclear and unhelpful.

Read and Improve Your Vocabulary: Make it a habit to read regularly to expand your language proficiency by exploring various reading materials, such as books and publications. It is important to learn new words and include them in your day-to-day dialogue as much as possible. This process expands your vocabulary and helps you communicate more strongly and coherently. Having a variety of words that you can use in your interactions enables you to communicate your message effectively.

Engage in Conversations: Take advantage of every opportunity to practice your communication skills in diverse settings. Boost your confidence by rehearsing challenging conversations with a friend or in front of a mirror.

Chapter 8

Effective Communication

in a Relationship

Sarah and John had previously struggled to understand one another because they often talked over each other and didn't listen carefully to what the other was saying. They decided to improve their communication skills by practicing active listening and using "I" statements during their discussions. They made a conscious effort to listen attentively without interrupting and to express their thoughts and feelings clearly. Over time, they observed improvements in their relationship, a greater ability to handle disagreements, and a deeper understanding of each other's perspectives.

Improving communication skills takes time and practice, but the benefits are well worth the effort. By being mindful of how you communicate and actively working on these skills, you can build stronger, more meaningful connections with others.

"I" statements are an excellent tool for communication because they allow you to express your feelings about what you want or need without placing blame on the other party. They are rooted in your emotions and help the other party understand your perspective. Here are some examples of "I" statements:

Expressing Feelings

"I feel hurt when you cancel our plans at the last minute."

"I feel appreciated when you acknowledge my efforts."

Expressing Needs

"I need some time to unwind after work."

"I would greatly appreciate your support when I'm feeling overwhelmed."

Expressing Preferences

"I prefer discussing essential issues in person rather than through text."

"I enjoy spending our weekends together without distractions."

Expressing Concerns

"I get anxious when you don't call to let me know you'll be late."

"I feel uncomfortable when we argue in front of the children."

Expressing Boundaries

"I need to set a boundary around our finances to avoid misunderstandings."

I need some personal space to rejuvenate.

Expressing Gratitude

"I appreciate your assistance with the household chores."

"I am thankful for your support during challenging times."

Structure of "I" Statements

To create effective "I" statements, use this structure: Start with "I":

Start your sentence with "I" to emphasize your feelings and experiences.

Describe the Behavior: Clearly outline the specific behaviors or situations impacting you.

Express Your Feelings: Explain how the behavior or situation impacts your emotions.

Specify Your Preference: Clearly articulate your needs or desires in the situation.

Example Structure

"I feel [emotion] when [the specific behavior]. I need [your need or preference]".

Real-Life Example

Scenario: Your partner often interrupts you during conversations, and it makes you feel unheard.

"I" Statement:

"I feel frustrated when I am interrupted during our conversations. I need to be able to finish my thoughts before you respond."

Using "I" statements can help you communicate more effectively and foster a more understanding and supportive relationship.

It's not uncommon for someone to react negatively when confronted with an "I" statement, especially if they feel defensive or caught off guard. Here are some strategies for handling adverse reactions and keeping the conversation productive.

Stay Calm and Composed

Take a Deep Breath: Before responding, pause, collect your thoughts, and avoid escalating the situation.

Acknowledge Their Feelings

Acknowledge and validate their feelings by showing understanding of their viewpoint. Show empathy. Ensure they know that their emotions are acknowledged and valued, nurturing a sense of trust and connection.

Example: "I can see that you're upset, and I understand why this could be tough to hear."

Maintain a Calm Tone: Keep your voice steady and calm to avoid escalating the situation.

Clarify Your Intentions

Reiterate Your Purpose: Remind them that your goal is to improve the relationship, not to blame or criticize.

Example: "I'm sharing this because I care about our relationship and want us to communicate better."

Listen Actively

Give Them Space to Express: Allow the other person to share their thoughts and feelings without interrupting.

Reflect: Paraphrase what they say to show that you are listening and to ensure you understand their perspective. Example: "It sounds like you're feeling hurt because you think I'm blaming you."

Stay Focused on the Issue

Avoid Getting Side-tracked: Keep the conversation focused on the specific issue at hand.

Address One Issue at a Time: Don't bring up multiple issues at once, as this can be overwhelming.

Use "We" Statements

Promote Teamwork: Shift the focus from "you vs. me" to "us working together." For example: "How can we work together to improve our communication?"

Take a Break if Needed

Pause the Conversation: If emotions are running high, suggest taking a break and revisiting the conversation later. Example: "Let's take a break and come back to this when we're both feeling calmer."

Seek Professional Help

Consider Counselling: If adverse reactions are frequent and challenging to manage, couples therapy or counseling can provide a neutral space to work through issues.

Real-Life Example

Scenario: You tell your partner, "I feel hurt when you cancel our plans at the last minute. I need more notice so I can adjust my schedule."

Adverse Reaction: Your partner responds defensively, "You always blame me for everything!"

Stay Calm: Take a deep breath and keep your tone calm.

Acknowledge Their Feelings: "I understand that you feel blamed, and that's not my intention."

Clarify Your Intentions: "I'm sharing this because I want us to have a better understanding and avoid misunderstandings in the future."

Engage Actively: "Could you elaborate on why you feel this way?" Keep Focus on the Issue: More importantly, let's discuss how we can respond with empathy and patience regarding the plans. This suggests that the speaker wants to diffuse the situation and promote more positive dialogue.

How To Improve Emotional Resilience

Improving emotional resilience can help you navigate life's challenges more effectively and maintain your well-being. Some strategies to enhance emotional resilience include:

Develop Self-Awareness

Understand Your Emotions: It's important to take some time to identify your feelings. Journaling is an effective way of writing down our feelings and the events that happened to us so we can better understand them.

Mindfulness Practices: It's advisable to practice mindfulness or meditation, as it allows you to be in the moment and connect deeply with your inner self.

Build Strong Relationships

Social Support: Develop a robust network of friends, family, and colleagues. Positive relationships offer emotional support and foster a sense of belonging.

Effective Communication: Building strong, meaningful connections begins with honest and open dialogue. Take time to sincerely express your thoughts and feelings while actively listening to others in return. Foster a safe environment where vulnerability is embraced and valued. When you show up authentically, you can trust and deepen your relationships. By practicing this, you strengthen your bond with others and create a space where trust and understanding can flourish.

Practice Self-Care: Self-care is the cornerstone of physical health and emotional resilience. Regular exercise, a balanced diet, proper hydration, and adequate rest are essential for physical health. Taking care of your physical health boosts your overall well-being and enhances your emotional health and resilience.

Embrace Relaxation Techniques: Explore relaxation methods that work for you, such as deep breathing, yoga, meditation, saying a short prayer, progressive muscle relaxation, or any element of rhythmic practices of ancient traditions. These approaches can help you manage stress, cultivate calmness, and bring a sense of peace and mindfulness into your daily life.

Transform Challenges into Opportunities: Each challenge offers an opportunity for growth. Change your mindset, focus on solutions, and move forward step by step. Embrace the lessons learned throughout the journey—every obstacle can make you stronger, wiser, and more resilient. Turn hardships into opportunities to grow and achieve success.

Develop Problem-Solving Skills: When challenges come your way, focus on what you can control. Break the problem into smaller, manageable steps, and tackle each one at your own pace with clarity and determination. Each small action builds confidence and brings you closer to a solution. Take it one step at a time.

Establish Goals: Set clear, attainable goals that truly reflect what is important to you. These objectives provide direction and a sense of purpose in life. As you progress, focus on cultivating a positive mindset to stay motivated and resilient. Every step you take brings you closer to a more meaningful and fulfilling existence.

Positive Thinking: Harness the power of positive thinking by nurturing a mindset of gratitude and focusing on what lies within your control. In difficult moments, take a step back and look for the silver linings—they're often hidden but can bring comfort and hope when you choose to notice them. By shifting your perspective, even hardships can reveal unexpected opportunities for growth and resilience.

Transform Negative Thoughts into Positivity: When negative thoughts hold you back, take a moment to question them. Ask yourself if they are merely assumptions. Then, reshape those thoughts into ones that encourage and empower you. Replace "I can't do this" with "I can..." or "I'm learning as I go." With practice, you can turn self-doubt into self-confidence and develop a mindset that fuels your growth.

Enhance Emotional Regulation: You can manage your emotions and maintain balance in your life. Begin by applying techniques such as reframing negative thoughts into positive ones. Cognitive restructuring, for instance, can assist you in shifting your perception and managing your emotions more effectively.

Practice Acceptance: Life doesn't always go as planned, and there are things we simply cannot change. Instead of resisting, practice acceptance—acknowledge what is beyond your control and free yourself from the stress of trying to change it. Then, shift your focus to what you can influence or improve.

Embrace Change and Adaptability: Life is full of twists and turns. By accepting and acknowledging the things you cannot control, you can free yourself from unnecessary stress and open the door to new possibilities. Adaptability is your strength—it enables you to navigate challenges and take charge of shaping your journey in a positive and meaningful way.

Flexibility: Flexibility enables you to manage and adapt to unexpected changes. Embrace new or uncertain situations with curiosity and an open mind. By remaining open and willing to adjust, you'll uncover strengths you didn't know you possessed and create opportunities for growth.

Learn from experience: Your past experiences hold valuable lessons that can guide you in the future. Take time to reflect on everything you've been through, both the successes and struggles, and identify the wisdom they've given you. These insights can help you grow stronger, equipping you to face future challenges with confidence.

Therapy and Counseling: Consider therapy and counseling, as they can help you better understand your emotions, manage stress, and build resilience. A skilled professional can also guide you through challenges, helping you navigate the complexities of life with confidence and clarity. Asking for support doesn't mean you're weak—it means you're brave enough to take steps toward growth and healing.

Life involves more than just getting through tough times; it's about truly living and growing. Take care of yourself, nurture meaningful relationships, and embrace opportunities to improve and challenge yourself. Every small effort contributes to a more balanced and fulfilling life, guiding you toward your best self. Keep striving—you're on a beautiful journey.

Chapter 9
Building Resilience
Through Mindfulness

A busy working woman, Jane faced considerable work pressure and various other challenges. She decided to adopt some mindfulness strategies in her daily life. Every morning, Jane took time to meditate and practice breathing techniques for at least 10 minutes. After a few weeks, Jane noted that she had gained a sense of calm and could manage stress more effectively. She also started writing in her journal to help monitor her emotions, develop emotional strength, and manage her feelings better. The practices Jane adopted may influence the experiences she faces in her daily life.

"Resilience is a muscle. Flex it enough, and it will take less effort to get over the emotional punches each time."

– Alecia Moore (Pink)

"The greatest glory in living lies not in never falling, but in rising every time we fall."
— Nelson Mandela

Building emotional resilience cannot be achieved in a single day. It is a process that requires awareness of oneself, others, and the environment, along with care and flexibility. However, cultivating this ability is achievable and can help prevent emotional breakdowns in professional and personal life.

Mindfulness

Mindfulness techniques can help you stay present, reduce stress, and improve your overall well-being. Here are some effective mindfulness practices you can incorporate into your daily routine.

Deep Breathing

How to Practice: Sit or lie down in a comfortable position. Close your eyes and take a deep breath through your nose, allowing your abdomen to expand. Exhale slowly through your mouth. Focus on the feeling of your breath coming in and out of your body.

Benefits: Deep breathing helps calm the mind, reduce anxiety, and improve focus.

Body Scan Meditation

How to Practice: Lie down or sit comfortably. Close your eyes and focus on your toes. Gradually shift your attention upward through your body, noting any sensations, tension, or areas of relaxation. Spend a few moments on each body part before progressing.

Benefits: This practice enhances body awareness, reduces stress, and encourages relaxation

Mindful Walking

How to Practice: Find a quiet place to walk. Focus on the sensation of your feet touching the ground, the movement of your legs, and the rhythm of your breathing. Observe your surroundings without judgment.

Benefits: Mindful walking can help clear your mind, enhance concentration, and connect you to the present moment.

Mindful Eating

How to Practice: During a meal, focus on the taste, texture, and aroma of your food. Eat slowly, savoring each bite. Pay attention to the sensations in your mouth and how your body feels as you eat.

Benefits: Mindful eating can enhance the enjoyment of food, boost digestion, and foster a healthier relationship with food.

Sitting Meditation

How to Practice: Sit comfortably with your back straight and hands resting in your lap. Close your eyes and focus on your breath. If your mind wanders, gently bring your attention back to your breath.

Benefits: Sitting meditation can improve emotional regulation, increase self-awareness, and reduce stress.

Mindful Listening

How to Practice: Choose a piece of music or a natural sound (like birds chirping or waves crashing). Close your eyes and focus entirely on the sound. Observe the various layers, tones, and rhythms without judgment.

Benefits: Mindful listening can enhance your auditory awareness, reduce stress, and improve your ability to focus.

Gratitude Practice

How to Practice: Take a few moments each day to reflect on things you are grateful for. You can write them down in a journal or simply think about them. Focus on the positive feelings associated with gratitude.

Benefits: Practicing gratitude can boost your mood, increase happiness, and improve overall well-being.

Mindful Journaling

How to Practice: Dedicate time each day to express your thoughts, feelings, and experiences through writing. Concentrate on the present moment and write without judgment. This can be an open-ended exercise or guided by specific prompts

Benefits: Mindful journaling can help you process emotions, increase self-awareness, and reduce stress.

Incorporating Mindfulness into Daily Life

Emma, a working woman, was overwhelmed by stress and her workload. She made an effort to incorporate mindfulness into her hectic daily routine. Each morning, she set aside five mindful minutes to savor her meals, focusing on the flavors and textures while taking deep breaths and going for a short walk around her neighborhood. In the evenings, she typically concentrated on being aware of the sights and sounds around her. These simple changes helped Emma feel more balanced and connected, allowing her to confront any challenges of the day.

Mindfulness techniques are versatile and can be practiced anywhere, anytime. Incorporating these practices into your daily routine can enhance your emotional resilience, reduce stress, and improve your overall well-being.

How Mindfulness Can Improve Sleep

Mindfulness can significantly improve sleep quality by calming the mind and reducing stress, which are common barriers to restful sleep. Here are some ways mindfulness can help:

Reducing Stress and Anxiety

Mindfulness practices, such as meditation and deep breathing, help activate the body's relaxation response, which counteracts the stress response. This can lower levels of cortisol, the stress hormone, making it easier to fall asleep and stay asleep.

Improving Sleep Quality

Mindfulness can enhance the overall quality of sleep by promoting deeper and more restorative sleep cycles. Techniques such as body scan meditation help relax the body and mind, preparing you for a restful night's sleep.

Breaking the Cycle of Insomnia

Mindfulness helps interrupt the cycle of insomnia by teaching you to observe your thoughts and feelings without judgment. This approach can lessen the anxiety and frustration that often accompany sleeplessness, making it easier to drift off.

Enhancing Emotional Regulation

Regular mindfulness practice can enhance emotional regulation, aiding you in managing worries and negative thoughts that may disrupt your sleep. By cultivating a sense of calm and acceptance, mindfulness makes it easier to release the stresses of the day.

Studies on Mindfulness Benefits

Numerous studies have demonstrated the benefits of mindfulness for both mental and physical health. Here are some key findings:

Mindfulness and Brain Changes

Harvard University research has shown that mindfulness meditation can lead to changes in brain structure. For example, an eight-week mindfulness program was found to increase the density of the hippocampus, which is involved in learning and memory, and reduce the size of the amygdala, which is responsible for stress and anxiety.

Reducing Symptoms of Depression and Anxiety

A review of over 200 studies found that mindfulness-based interventions, such as Mindfulness-Based Stress Reduction (MBSR) and Mindfulness-Based Cognitive Therapy (MBCT), are effective at reducing symptoms of depression and anxiety. These interventions helped individuals in managing their thoughts and emotions more effectively.

Improving Physical Health

Mindfulness has been shown to have various physical health benefits, including lowering blood pressure, improving immune function, and reducing chronic pain. Studies suggest that mindfulness can help manage conditions like irritable bowel syndrome, fibromyalgia, and psoriasis.

Mindfulness for Better Sleep

For years, Lisa struggled with insomnia. She often lay down and remained awake for hours, worrying about work and personal issues. To improve her sleep, she decided to try mindfulness meditation. Each night, she practiced a body scan meditation, focusing on relaxing each part of her body. Over time, Lisa noticed that she fell asleep more quickly and woke up feeling more rested. The mindfulness practice helped her let go of her worries and created a sense of calm that made it easier to sleep.

Mindfulness is a powerful tool for improving sleep by reducing stress, enhancing emotional regulation, and promoting relaxation. However, the benefits of mindfulness extend beyond sleep, positively affecting mental and physical health. By incorporating mindfulness practices into your daily routine, you can enjoy better sleep and improved overall well-being.

Chapter 10

Final Thoughts

Final Thoughts on Love

The journey of love is a continuous discovery, growth, and connection process. Here are some final thoughts to consider as you navigate this journey:

Embrace the Journey: Love is not just about reaching a destination but enjoying the journey itself. Embrace each stage and the experience it brings.

Be Patient: Relationships take time to develop and mature. Be patient with yourself and your partner as you grow together.

Celebrate the Moments: Celebrate the small and big moments in your relationship. These celebrations strengthen your bond and create lasting memories.

Stay Committed: Commitment is a choice you make every day. Stay dedicated to nurturing your relationship and supporting each other.

Seek Support: If you ever find yourself in a difficult situation or need support, is it okay to ask your friends, family, clergy, or other professionals for help. Having people around you to encourage and support you can also help you avoid or deal with issues that may arise in your relationship.

Understanding the stages of love, communicating effectively, and working on your personal growth and that of your partner is essential for building a strong, lasting relationship. Love is one of life's most remarkable experiences, and being in a relationship makes it even more special and memorable. It is a fulfilling experience that enhances your life while adding joy and meaning to your relationships.

Family as the School of Love

The family is often viewed as the first environment where we begin to understand and experience love and relationships. It serves as a foundational space for expressing and nurturing different forms of love—such as affection, care, and empathy. By exploring the various stages of love within the family context, we can better understand its crucial role in shaping our emotional growth and relationship skills.

Parental Love

Parental love is the first form of love that a child experiences. It is characterized by the following:

Unconditional Support: Parents are the fundamental and most important figures in a child's life. They provide unconditional support for the child's physical, emotional, and psychological needs.

Guidance and Protection: Parents assist children in navigating different aspects of life, safeguard them from harm, and provide a sense of security and trust.

Role Modelling: Parents are the most influential figures in a child's life. Children see their parents as superheroes and role models. They learn to love, show empathy, express compassion, be good to their neighbors, and be responsible citizens in their communities. They observe their parents and gain valuable lessons from them.

Sibling Love

The second stage is the sibling love stage, during which children start showing affection toward their siblings and other family members, including cousins, uncles, and aunts.

This stage involves:

Shared Experiences: Families with siblings allow children the opportunity to learn from one another, enjoy fun times, and offer mutual support, thus developing close friendships.

Conflict and Resolution: While it is common knowledge that siblings often fight, they are also the best teachers when it comes to resolving conflicts, making concessions, and forgiving each other.

Mutual Support: Siblings often support each other emotionally and practically, fostering a sense of loyalty and solidarity.

Conjugal Love

Cultural definitions of love encompass the ideal romantic and marital relationship between partners. They pertain to love within a marital context characterized by companionship, comfort, and security. This type of love is also referred to as realistic love.

This stage involves:

Partnership and Commitment: A marriage is built on mutual commitment, love, trust, and a shared goal of creating a life together. Mutual trust means that both individuals in a relationship have confidence in one another.

Mutual Trust: Both couples involved in a relationship trust that the other person will not deceive, cheat, or betray their confidence. It means believing your partner has your best interests at heart, will not let you down, and will not lie to you. This trust is earned over time through actions and words.

Emotional and Physical Intimacy: Partners engage in sexual experiences and cultivate emotional closeness, which strengthens their relationship.

Growth and Adaptation: It is a common saying that couples are meant to grow old together. This means that as they navigate through different phases of life and overcome challenges, they become more united. They support each other's growth and strive toward the same goals and purpose.

In practice, there are many ways to express love. Family is fundamentally the school of love, where we learn the essential tools and principles of affection, empathy, sharing, and conflict resolution within unique familial relationships that may differ from one another.

Foundation of Values: Children develop essential values such as respect, kindness, and empathy within a family, which are necessary for building strong relationships.

Lifelong Bonds: The connections formed within the family are typically lifelong, providing a continuous source of encouragement, affection, support and identity.

Learning and Growth: Family relationships provide opportunities for learning and development. They teach us how to build connections with others and manage our emotions. Family relationships also play a significant role in children's social development, teaching them values, respect, and responsibility.

Resilience and Strength: Family love and support foster resilience and fortitude in people, enabling them to confront life's trials with assurance.

Viewing the family as a school of love helps us appreciate the values we have learned and how they can be applied to other relationships. Whether it's parental, sibling, or conjugal love, each stage enriches our understanding of love and aids us in forming positive and healthy relationships throughout every stage of life.

Final Thoughts on Marriage

Marriage, like any other important decision in one's life, is a choice that should not be taken lightly. Even in today's world of social media, love, commitment, and partnership do not lose their values and importance. Here are some final thoughts to consider.

Be True to Yourself: Authenticity is key in any relationship. Be honest about your needs, desires, and boundaries, and encourage your partner to do the same.

Invest in Your Relationship: Make time for one another, nurture your bond, and prioritize your relationship. Successful marriages are beautiful and require continuous nurturing and effort to ensure their longevity

Embrace Change Together: Life is not always easy and is constantly changing. Face these changes together, and you will support each other during both good times and bad.

Celebrate Milestones: It is always important to enjoy joyful occasions and accomplishments in a relationship. These happy building blocks help foster the relationship and contribute to the creation of even more cherished moments.

Seek Help When Needed: If you have any concerns, do not hesitate to seek professional assistance. Local clergy, counseling, and therapy can be beneficial in addressing these issues. Marriage and family therapy can be an especially helpful experience.

Understanding the processes involved in building relationships, learning from past experiences, and accepting the necessity of change are crucial for maintaining healthy and satisfying relationships in the future. Marriage is a partnership that thrives on mutual respect, love, and commitment, and with the right approach, it can be one of the most rewarding experiences of your life.

Final Thoughts on Divorce

Going through a divorce is one of life's significant challenges that presents an opportunity for growth. To effectively manage the intricacies of divorce, and emerge resilient from this time, familiarize yourself with the dimensions at play, and reach out for support when needed. Focus your efforts on rebuilding your life in a meaningful way. Finally, here are some closing thoughts to consider as you move forward.

Embrace Change: Although change can sometimes be challenging to confront, it also brings positive transformation. Take pleasure in the opportunity to start anew and strive to achieve objectives.

Prioritize Self-Care: It is essential to take care of your physical and emotional well-being. Engage in activities that bring you joy and relaxation.

Set Realistic Goals: Set achievable goals for your personal and professional life. Celebrate small victories along the way.

Stay Positive: Maintaining a positive outlook is important to effectively handle the challenges of divorce. Focus on the new life that lies ahead and the opportunities it presents. This means you should strive to stay positive even during divorce, as this can help you see it as a new chapter in your life rather than something negative.

Thank you for joining me on this journey of love, marriage, and divorce. I wish you well as you navigate your own path, and may you be blessed with wisdom, growth, and purpose.

AFTERWORD

As we conclude this exploration of love, marriage, and divorce, it's important to reflect on the valuable lessons we've learned along the way. Relationships, in all their forms, are intricate and multifaceted, offering both joy and challenges. Here are some key insights and takeaways:

Communication is Key: Open, honest, and respectful communication forms the foundation of any healthy relationship. Expressing feelings, needs, and concerns clearly is crucial while actively listening to your partner.

Mutual Respect and Understanding: Respecting each other's individuality and embracing differences can strengthen the bond. It's important to appreciate your partner's perspective and support their growth.

Adaptability and Compromise: This means that relationships require some give and take, and couples must be willing to change. Navigating these changes in life can help you build a stronger relationship with your partner.

Self-love and Personal Growth: It is very important to have one's identity and develop as an individual. In a healthy relationship, each partner should be allowed and encouraged to follow his or her own path.

Conflict Resolution is very important because conflicts are bound to arise from time to time, but how such conflicts are solved can make a huge difference. Solving problems in a relationship by focusing on finding solutions rather than assigning blame can go a long way toward saving the relationship and even strengthening it.

Forgiveness and Letting Go: Rejection is painful, and the burden of holding grudges is even worse. Forgiveness can help individuals release feelings of anger and resentment toward those who may have caused them harm, which is essential for personal growth, particularly in relationships or after a breakup. Having a support network, with friends and family by your side, can offer comfort and guidance during times of crisis.

Embracing Change: Life and relationships are dynamic, not fixed. Seeing change as a positive experience instead of a negative one can enrich the journey.

Love and Compassion: Love and compassion are among the most important building blocks that strengthen and define relationships. One may encounter challenges in these areas. Developing qualities of acceptance and closure is vital. In the case of divorce, it is crucial to come to terms with the situation and find closure regarding various aspects. Divorce serves as an opportunity to pause and reflect, improve oneself, and look forward to the future.

Experiencing love, marriage, and divorce is profoundly personal. Each relationship teaches us something unique and shapes our personalities and preferences in partners. As we move forward, carrying these lessons with us, we become better equipped to build and maintain happier, stronger relationships. Every blessing or challenge we face contributes to our growth as individuals and partners, allowing us to cultivate a deeper, more genuine appreciation for what love truly means.

Leave a one-click review

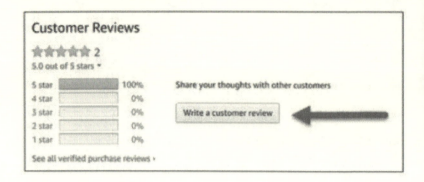

I would be truly grateful if you could take just 60 seconds to write a review on Amazon, even if it's only a few sentences.

Made in the USA
Columbia, SC
30 May 2025

58714342R00098